Gri... ...ed the airstrip,
div...

The a... prior to its left, slowing as its side
door flew open and a figure jumped to the ground.
Thin streams of red tracer rounds zoomed upward.

"Whoever the hell that guy is," Grimaldi said over
the radio, "I'm taking fire, and it's coming close!"

Bolan paused, sighted the hostile gunner and
squeezed off a quick burst. The man twisted in
Bolan's direction, and the Executioner fired again.
His target jerked slightly. He was hit—but how
badly?

Seconds later he had his answer as the red tracer
rounds began zipping past him. He ducked, rolled
to the left and came up on one knee just as the firing
stopped. He saw the hostile leaning back, his right
arm extended behind him.

Bolan fired another burst, and seconds later the flash
and concussion of an explosion washed over him,
accompanied by a second, larger conflagration as
the plane went up in a gigantic fireball.

MACK BOLAN ®
The Executioner

THE EXECUTIONER®

DON PENDLETON'S

MISSILE INTERCEPT

A GOLD EAGLE BOOK FROM
W🦅RLDWIDE®

TORONTO • NEW YORK • LONDON
AMSTERDAM • PARIS • SYDNEY • HAMBURG
STOCKHOLM • ATHENS • TOKYO • MILAN
MADRID • WARSAW • BUDAPEST • AUCKLAND

First edition June 2016

ISBN-13: 978-0-373-64447-6

Special thanks and acknowledgment to
Michael A. Black for his contribution to this work.

Missile Intercept

Recycling programs
for this product may
not exist in your area.

Printed in U.S.A.

It is only those who have neither fired a shot nor heard the shrieks and groans of the wounded who cry aloud for blood, more vengeance, more desolation.
—William Tecumseh Sherman

There is nothing pretty about a nuclear conflagration. Yet the insanity continues. Images of Hiroshima and Nagasaki should serve to stay the hand of all leaders. But they don't. We must stand strong and protect the innocents.
—Mack Bolan

THE
MACK BOLAN
LEGEND

Nothing less than a war could have fashioned the destiny of the man called Mack Bolan. Bolan earned the Executioner title in the jungle hell of Vietnam.

But this soldier also wore another name—Sergeant Mercy. He was so tagged because of the compassion he showed to wounded comrades-in-arms and Vietnamese civilians.

Mack Bolan's second tour of duty ended prematurely when he was given emergency leave to return home and bury his family, victims of the Mob. Then he declared a one-man war against the Mafia.

He confronted the Families head-on from coast to coast, and soon a hope of victory began to appear. But Bolan had broken society's every rule. That same society started gunning for this elusive warrior—to no avail.

So Bolan was offered amnesty to work within the system against terrorism. This time, as an employee of Uncle Sam, Bolan became Colonel John Phoenix. With a command center at Stony Man Farm in Virginia, he and his new allies—Able Team and Phoenix Force—waged relentless war on a new adversary: the KGB.

But when his one true love, April Rose, died at the hands of the Soviet terror machine, Bolan severed all ties with Establishment authority.

Now, after a lengthy lone-wolf struggle and much soul-searching, the Executioner has agreed to enter an "arm's-length" alliance with his government once more, reserving the right to pursue personal missions in his Everlasting War.

Prologue

Palatial Garden near Kim Il Sung Square
Pyongyang, North Korea

Colonel Yi Sun-Shin of the Korean People's Army of the
Democratic People's Republic of Korea watched as Gumon
Yoong, the Black Dragon, stalked his last two opponents.
Ten bodies littered the ground between them. The Dragon,
clad in his dark special forces military fatigues, had dispatched the others with a series of deft blows, punches,
whirling kicks and chopping strikes with the edge of his
hand.

At least these executions were more entertaining than
the last batch, Yi thought. Those had been carried out with
an antiaircraft gun, leaving the hapless general and his assistant little more than misshapen piles of bones and flesh
on the firing range. It was like using a sledgehammer to
smash a mouse.

One of the Dragon's remaining opponents assumed a
fighting stance, his fists outstretched.

The Dragon smirked, continuing his steady advance.

His opponent lurched forward and threw a high roundhouse kick, which the Dragon brushed away with a casual flick of his hand.

The man twisted, executing a spinning back kick.

Instead of blocking the blow, the Dragon stepped inside the arc of the kick, letting his opponent's leg curl around him. The Dragon's hands were a blur as they struck the man's exposed neck, the tandem blows leaving his head flopping like a broken doll's. He slipped to the ground, a trail of blood leaking from a corner of his mouth, his eyes open and sightless.

The Dragon's last opponent glanced around nervously, but the stone walls of the garden were high. There was no place to flee, yet he tried, turning and running away at full speed. The Dragon pursued him, closing the gap easily and then leaping into the air, his left leg tucked, the right cocked and ready. The Dragon's right foot shot out, clipping the back of the running man's neck. He fell face-first onto the hard ground as the Dragon landed lightly on his feet.

After grunts of approval, the country's leader and his entourage stood and filed out of the garden without so much as a word, heading to the front of the building for the commencement of the Victory Day parade.

Yi surveyed the carnage. The last remaining members of the freighter that had been seized in the Panama Canal now lay dead. Such was the price of failure in the march toward victory. Yi glanced at his watch. It had taken the Dragon just over three minutes to dispatch them all.

The colonel knew his fate would be similar if he failed in his mission. It had been a warning as well as an example. "The bungling incompetents have disgraced us with their failure," his immediate supervisor, General Song Hai-Son, had said. "They will be dealt with immediately prior to the parade, and then our supreme commander will be informed of your coming mission."

The juxtaposition of the two events was not lost on Yi. Mission failure was not an option. Any outcome except total and complete success would be considered an affront to their leader's authority, and whether the transgression was real or imagined did not matter. To fail was a death sentence.

"Colonel Yi," a voice called from the arched doorway.

He turned and saw General Song standing by the ornately fashioned arch. Yi approached him, stopped, came to attention and saluted.

"Yes, General."

Song snapped his fingers at the soldier standing beside him. The man remained at attention, motionless.

"Go tell our supreme commander we will soon be on our way," the general ordered.

The soldier saluted, replied in the affirmative and left with crack precision.

"The Black Dragon looks ready for the coming task," Song said.

"He is always ready, sir," Yi replied. "As am I."

Song nodded and grunted his approval. "Good. Come, let us proceed to the balcony. The Victory Day parade is about to begin."

He began walking slowly down the long hallway toward the elevators.

"I have gone over your plan," the general said. "I have some concerns." His face puckered into an expression of displeasure. "It seems overly complicated."

Yi had expected as much. Their current leader, like those before him, had surrounded himself with men essentially lacking in both cunning and guile, in an apparent attempt to minimize disloyalty and the possibility of deceit. Thus, military tactics had been degraded to the most basic. Such limited imagination engendered incompetence.

The colonel knew if he were to say that to Song, it would

be tantamount to holding a pistol to his own temple. Instead, he applied a bit of deference.

"I agree, General, that it is complicated, but may I remind you that it is as you have said in the past. The clever warrior uses subterfuge and deception to minimize his expenditures and maximize his strengths."

The general lifted an eyebrow, appeared to contemplate, and then smiled fractionally.

Yi had fictitiously attributed the dictum to Song, but also knew the false attribution would be welcomed and accepted by the vain officer. Yi's father, who had fought the Americans decades before, had taught his son the lessons of war and of mastering an opponent. Deception was imperative in both instances.

"When I was a young boy," Yi continued, "growing up in the military camp near the DMZ, there was an old man who would amuse the soldiers with a game using three walnut half shells. A shell game."

Song's eyes narrowed. He said nothing.

"The man would place a dried pea under one of the shells, then move them around. The soldiers would try to guess under which one they would find the pea. They would wager on it."

The general's visage twisted into a scowl. "They were gambling?"

"Only with cigarettes." That was basically true, because none of the soldiers had any money, but Yi left that part out. "But the man with the walnut shells would never lose." Yi paused. "The dried pea was concealed in his hand the entire time, and was never truly placed under one of the shells."

The general's eyes widened. "Deception."

"The principle is the same in this instance," Yi said. "The three ships are under way."

"And the other?" Song asked. "The Iranian?"

"Some of our agents are with it now. Soon the Black Dragon and I will be under way, as well."

"I do not trust these Iranians," Song said, his face puckering again. "Such religious fanaticism hardly inspires trust or reliability."

"They hate the Americans," Yi replied. "And as the saying goes, the enemy of our enemy is our friend." He knew the deal of appearing to share their nuclear capabilities with Iran was a necessary evil. For all their failings as a culture, they had the one redeeming feature that made the association necessary: money.

The two men reached an elevator and entered. The doors closed and the elevator car ascended. As they rode upward, Yi wondered if his story had achieved its purpose. Seconds later, he knew it had.

"Subterfuge and deception," the general repeated, smiling now.

Yi smiled, too. He had assuaged Song's doubts about the plan. All that remained now was the implementation, and the new era would begin.

"I trust that your travels will be both expeditious and fruitful," Song said.

The elevator doors opened, and Yi could hear the cheers from the crowd below through the portals of the balconies. He could not help but feel a swell of pride as he anticipated the procession of marching soldiers, the lines of tanks and the massive array of intercontinental ballistic missiles. The people's army, his army, was ready to fight to the death on command, each man's leg kicking outward in precise unison with the others, their AK-47s held at port arms without deviance, their faces turning as they passed the buildings. Yi felt the surge of pride in his army, his country…

Another set of missiles passed, and Yi knew that soon the Americans would be driven off the lower peninsula forever, once the ICBMs were transformed into the new dragon ships, once they had the technology capable of maintaining the missile trajectory upon reentry to the atmosphere.

Soon, he thought, the world would bow before North Korea's might. The puppets in the South would be overthrown, and not even the Chinese, who had for so long cast their dominant shadow over the Korean peninsula, would be an equal.

He closed his eyes and pictured the long-ago sea vessels, a huge dragon's head rising from the armored bow of each, striking fear into the hearts of the hated Japanese and Chinese. These vessels, once the most powerful ships to roam the seas, had been conceived and piloted by his ancient namesake, Yi Sun-Shin. Soon these new dragon ships would restore his country to its proper place of prominence. It would be one Korea, unified and under Communist rule, no longer a small fish dominated by whales.

Soon...

1

Culiacán, Sinaloa, Mexico

Mack Bolan, aka the Executioner, and his team were spread out in the darkness along the tree line, about thirty yards from the high cyclone fence that surrounded the facility. The remote grounds, once the site of a Jesuit monastery, now housed a warehouse for the Sinaloa Cartel. Just outside the fence were the crumbling ruins of the old church.

The Executioner gently tapped the bottom of the magazine inserted into his Heckler & Koch MP-5 to make sure it was properly seated, then checked the tape that secured the inverted second magazine to the first. His weapon was ready.

Aerial photos had given them the layout of the place, a metal, prefab building approximately one hundred yards in length, set on a concrete slab and surrounded by the cyclone fence. A short, curving road led to a paved airstrip on the west side of the compound. Once Bolan and his team were through the fence, they would have to cross a wide courtyard with little cover to get to the warehouse.

An informant had told the authorities that trucks would

be loaded that night with marijuana, cocaine and brown heroin. The green light for the raid had been given less than an hour earlier, and the team had been hustled to the airstrip to be transported to the remote site. The highway was a scant quarter mile from the compound, and they'd double-timed it all the way to the tree line.

Bolan glanced at his watch: 0252. It was as good a time as any for a raid, he thought, and keyed his mic to Jack Grimaldi's frequency. "Jack, do you copy?"

"Your eye in the sky is waiting for the show to start, Sarge," the Stony Man pilot replied from the helicopter high above. "I've got your back."

"We're almost in position," Bolan said.

"Roger that. Want me to do another flyover?"

Before Bolan could answer he heard the drone of an aircraft engine. He looked upward, but was unable to see the sky through the thick canopy.

"Sounds like a plane approaching," he said. "See anything?"

It took Grimaldi a few seconds to reply. "Roger. Looks like a twin-engine craft coming in from the east. I'd better drop back and down for a bit."

Bolan knew that Grimaldi was blacked out and now positioning his helicopter to minimize the chance of being spotted by anyone in the plane. It was a reasonable assumption that the aircraft was going to land on the airstrip located on the other side of the building.

Bolan clicked his mic in reply just as Sergeant Jesus Martinez, the team leader of the Mexican marines, tapped him on the shoulder.

"What does your friend in the helicopter say?" he asked. The dark camo paint on his face was shiny with sweat.

"An aircraft is coming. Un…avión, ah, viene," Bolan said in broken Spanish, for the benefit of Captain Ruiz, who was next to Martinez and had a limited knowledge of English.

The two men could not have appeared more different physically. Ruiz was handsome and lean, while the bulky Martinez looked like an aging heavyweight past his prime and gone to seed. The two bent close and whispered together, their words too soft for Bolan to discern, even though he had deliberately kept his fluency in Spanish to himself.

Martinez smiled and nodded. *"Bueno."* He whispered again to Ruiz, then turned back to Bolan. "Perhaps we will catch some fish this time, eh, my friend?"

Bolan assessed the most prudent move, considering the unexpected development of the approaching plane. He and Grimaldi had been assigned as "civilian assistants" to the Mexican marines for this raid. US government personnel had been regularly assisting the Mexican authorities with raids on the cartel locations, but an FBI agent had been wounded during the last one, sending up a red flag in Washington. US participation was supposed to be covert, their agents not directly involved in hazardous situations without official sanction, but things were moving at such a fast pace that clandestine ops had been ordered to cut through the miles of red tape. Now, while the various agencies braced for a full and transparent hearing and investigation on the Hill, the President had contacted Hal Brognola, director of the Sensitive Operations Group based at Stony Man Farm, to assist in this latest interdiction effort.

So here they were, Grimaldi dropping off the assault team in the vicinity and playing guardian angel in an old beat-up Huey, without armament, and Bolan on the ground with an unfamiliar group of Mexican marines.

"Looks like they're lighting up for a landing," Grimaldi's

voice said in Bolan's ear mic. "A van just exited the front gate, heading toward the strip."

The Executioner turned to Martinez and suggested they move into the old ruins and send two men to cut a hole in the fence during the distraction of the plane landing. Martinez agreed and dispatched the men. It took them less than five minutes to accomplish the task, and in the interim Bolan heard the sound of the plane's tires touching down.

Grimaldi confirmed the landing and said he was still blacked out, but ascending to a better vantage point.

"Jack, stay far enough out so they don't hear you," Bolan said, keying his mic.

"Roger."

Bolan and Martinez took cover by a dilapidated wall that had long ago been the front of the church as the rest of the twelve-man team filtered through the ruins, taking up their positions. Bolan flipped down his night-vision goggles and surveyed the scene. Everything looked clear at the rear of the compound. He knew at least one man was stationed at the guard post by the front gate, and two others in watchtowers strategically placed at the far corners.

"The plane's on the ground," Grimaldi said over the radio. "Several subjects getting out. The van's picking them up... I'm counting five total."

"We move now," Bolan said.

Martinez keyed his mic and issued the order. After pausing to cross himself, he pulled his mask up to cover the lower portion of his face, then moved to the door.

Ruiz nodded to both of them. His mask hung loosely around his neck, and he had declined camo paint, indicating that he was not going to be an active participant in the raid.

Bolan ducked through the opening, then sprinted toward the gaping hole in the fence. The two cutters had done an excellent job. The Executioner veered left, as was their plan. He knew Martinez would go right, each man alternating until they were at the corners of the prefab building. Bolan crouched and took a quick look around the corner.

Two guards kicked a soccer ball back and forth. Their rifles, AR-15s from the look of them, were slung casually across their bodies.

Hopefully, these guys were into their game, Bolan thought. The prospect of facing automatic-rifle fire made the situation a bit more problematic.

At least the watchtower on this side appeared empty. Bolan sent two men to verify. After checking the location of the soccer-playing guards, the two marines raced across the expanse to the bottom of the guard tower. One man climbed its ladder as the other one covered him. Moments later, the one at the top signaled that it was clear.

Mistake number one for the bad guys, Bolan thought. He relayed the information to Martinez.

"Looks like the van's heading away from the airstrip and back toward the main gate," Grimaldi said over the radio.

Bolan acknowledged and relayed that information to Martinez, as well. The original plan called for covert infiltration and possibly taking prisoners for interrogation, but Bolan wasn't hopeful on that count. They were going into the belly of the beast. Resistance and gunplay were almost always a given. These weren't the kind of men who surrendered without a fight. If they did, they'd surely face the wrath of the cartel bosses afterward.

"The tower on this side looks deserted," Martinez said.

That seemed exceptionally lax, which was great news for the marines, if their good fortune was to be believed.

"I am sending two men to check the front tower and secure the corner," Martinez whispered over the radio.

"Roger," Bolan answered.

With the watchtower positions neutralized, and two men

positioned at the front of the building, the rest of the raid should go like clockwork, Bolan thought. He tested the fit of the sound suppressor on his MP-5 and got ready to round the corner and take out the two sentries on his side.

Grimaldi's voice was a whisper in Bolan's ear mic. "The van's coming in the gate. The overhead door's going up in front."

The Executioner informed Martinez.

Almost time, Bolan thought. Let them start to disembark from the vehicle and then we can hit them hard.

"The van's inside," Grimaldi's voice said over the radio. "The big door's closing."

Bolan keyed his mic. "Is everybody in position?" After hearing the affirmative clicks, he said, "Get ready to move."

The soccer ball suddenly bounced past him, and the labored breathing of a man running became audible.

As the guard ran past, chasing the errant ball, Bolan reached out in the darkness and grabbed him, slamming him to the ground. He grunted and started to yell, but the Executioner brought down two hammer-fist blows on the fallen man's temple. Satisfied he was out cold, Bolan told one of the marines to secure him, and stood, just as a voice from the other side of the building called out in Spanish, "The marines are here! The marines are here!"

Seconds later a siren began to wail, followed by staccato bursts of gunfire. It had to be the cartel guards firing, as Bolan and all the marines had sound suppressors attached to their weapons. Floodlights positioned along the fence blazed on, illuminating the night.

Bolan closed his eyes briefly and ripped off his night-vision goggles to avoid being temporarily blinded. He took another quick look around the corner. The fallen guard's soccer partner, his rifle at the ready, was running toward Bolan's position. The Executioner brought up the barrel of the MP-5, poked it around the building and squeezed off a three-round burst. The running guard jerked spasmodically, then crumpled to the ground.

The Executioner raced forward, shooting out the closest floodlight. The marine under the guard tower joined him, and Bolan knew Martinez and his three men were advancing on the other side. They had to get to the front of the building and take control of the situation.

The second floodlight along the fence line exploded and went dark. Bolan figured the marine in the tower was taking them out to cover the advance of his teammates. He had an M-16, which gave him greater range.

Ahead, two more cartel guards appeared around the corner, the red flashes of their firing weapons bright blossoms in the darkness. Bolan veered left as several rounds zipped by him. One of the marines fell.

Bolan brought the MP-5 to his shoulder and fired two three-round bursts at the cartel guards. Both men danced and twisted, silhouetted by the final set of floodlights as they dropped to the ground.

"Front gate and tower secure," Martinez said over the radio.

Intel had estimated the number of hostiles to be between ten and fifteen, more if one of the cartel bosses was on-site. One could be aboard the incoming plane, in which case Bolan's team could momentarily be facing a more substantial force. He slowed as they closed in on the front of the building. It was time to take out the remaining floodlights.

The Executioner took aim and shot the last two lights. Despite the ringing in his ears, he heard a mechanical squeal and knew that the big overhead door was rising.

Keying his mic, he checked with Martinez. "You might have trouble coming out the front end."

"We have the front secured," Martinez said over the

radio, sounding breathless. "The van went inside. We are—
Mierda!"

Bolan glanced around the corner and heard the sound of
a metal-on-metal ripping crash as the van barreled through
the opening, scraping the bottom of the rising door and
sideswiping the door frame.

Martinez's crew began firing at the vehicle. Bolan
ducked back, avoiding a cross fire. The blasts of loud automatic fire emanated from the van, which continued toward
the front gate. Bolan fired off a burst at it, then realized
the futility and ceased.

"Send two of your men after it," Bolan said into his mic.
"The rest of us need to secure the warehouse. Perimeter
containment, hold your positions."

Two marines from Martinez's team broke off toward
the airstrip. Bolan motioned the man next to him to follow,
then slipped through the open overhead door and headed
to the right. The warehouse was fully lit and he could see
three cartel guards running forward, sweeping the area in
front of them with autofire.

Bolan stopped behind a section of rooms jutting from
the wall. Several rounds pierced the wood and plaster-
board. Bolan knew that his position offered only a modicum of cover and little concealment. His adversaries
obviously knew where he was. Martinez surged forward,
his MP-5 spitting out rounds. The cartel guards switched
their aim, giving Bolan the momentary respite he needed
to zero in on them with a pair of short bursts of fire. Two
fell almost simultaneously, and as the third cartel guard
switched his rifle back toward Bolan, Martinez popped
up and shot the man.

Aside from the crudely constructed rooms along the
eastern wall, the warehouse was basically free of obstruc-
tions. Some packaged items were stacked on the opposite
side, and four box trucks were parked in the center aisle.

Another cartel guard leaned around the corner of one of the trucks and brought up his weapon, but before he could fire, the Executioner sent a zipping stitch of rounds across the man's chest. He tumbled forward. Across the room, Martinez and his team brought down two more hostiles.

An eerie silence descended over the room. Bolan, Martinez and the rest of the marines continued to clear the warehouse, encountering no apparent resistance.

Grimaldi's voice sounded in Bolan's ear mic. "There's a firefight going on at the airstrip. Looks like that plane is turning around for a takeoff."

Bolan glanced at Martinez. "There's trouble at the airstrip."

"Go! We've got this one covered."

The Executioner nodded and worked his way outside, moving with caution and deliberation toward the airstrip as he inserted a fresh magazine into his weapon. Ahead, he could see flashes of gunfire. The twin propellers of the plane were spinning with increasing power as the aircraft started to move.

"Want me to do a flyover to try to keep them on the ground?" Grimaldi asked.

"Go for it," Bolan said.

Grimaldi buzzed the airstrip, flying directly in the path of the accelerating plane.

The craft jerked to the left, slowing appreciably. The side door flew open and a figure jumped to the ground. Thin streams of red fire zoomed upward.

Tracer rounds, Bolan figured.

The bodies of two marines lay in the field before him. No time to check them now, he thought. He was almost to the airfield.

"Whoever the hell that guy is," Grimaldi said over the radio, "he can shoot. I'm taking fire, and it's coming close."

Bolan paused, acquired a sight picture of the hostile and

squeezed off a quick burst. The man twisted in his direction, and the Executioner saw that he was Asian. Bolan fired again, and his target jerked slightly.

He was hit. The question was, how badly?

Seconds later the Executioner had his answer as red tracer rounds began zipping past him. He ducked, rolled to the left and came up on one knee just as the firing stopped. He acquired a sight picture and saw the hostile leaning back, his right arm extended behind him.

Grenade, Bolan thought, and didn't hesitate. He shot the man, and seconds later the flash and concussion of an explosion washed over him, accompanied by a second, larger conflagration as the plane went up in a gigantic fireball.

Bolan keyed his mic and asked Martinez for a sitrep.

"We are secure inside," the sergeant replied. "One prisoner."

"Casualties?" Bolan asked.

"One of my men wounded. One KIA." Martinez's voice cracked when he said the last part. "Captain Ruiz has called for a medevac, and reinforcements to take control."

Bolan frowned. Too many casualties. This had been a debacle.

He radioed Grimaldi, saying they had a wounded marine, and asking if he could set the chopper on the airstrip.

"No problem," the pilot said. "You just get that marine over to me and I'll fly him out."

Bolan radioed the information to Martinez, who offered his thanks for Grimaldi's assistance.

After the wounded man had been loaded into the chopper, with another of his comrades to direct the flight, Grimaldi lifted off.

Bolan tagged up with Martinez, who was standing near the rest of the team. A man in a bright orange short-sleeved shirt sat in the middle, his hands fastened behind his back, a briefcase on the floor in front of him. He was whistling softly, and when Martinez told him to shut up, he kept on whistling. Enraged, the sergeant walked over and slapped him across the face.

"Is that the best you can do?" the seated man asked in Spanish, then spit on the floor. "You are the dirt beneath my feet."

Martinez cocked his hand back to deliver another blow.

"Sounds like he's trying to get to you," Bolan said. "He's trying to bait you."

"You are American?" the prisoner asked in English, looking at Bolan. "Yeah, you must be. You don't have a mask on, like these cowards."

Martinez kept his arm cocked for a few moments more, the expression of fury locked on his face, then he slowly lowered his hand and joined Bolan.

He leaned close and said in English, "I think he's Cuban, from the sound of him."

Bolan had the same thought, noticing the Cuban inflection.

"Yeah, you're right, chief," the prisoner said. "I am Cuban. And now let me talk to the man in charge."

"I am in charge here," Martinez said, turning toward him. "What do you want?"

"Not you," the Cuban said. "The American. I've got information to trade. No way you can give me what I want."

"And what might that be?" Bolan asked.

The Cuban leaned back and smirked. "A condo in Miami for starters." He laughed. "You're gonna be interested in what I've got to say."

Bolan said nothing.

The Cuban smirked again. "American, you're not gonna believe what I've got. No way. But it's big. Real big."

Bolan watched the man sitting there smiling, a look of total confidence on his face.

This could be interesting, he thought.

NIISA Headquarters
Adobe Flats, New Mexico

JAMES HUDSON WATCHED from the back of the auditorium. Dr. Phillip McGreagor, as he liked to be called, stood on the stage holding the microphone like a rock star, gesturing toward the ceiling-to-floor screen behind him as it depicted the white, streamlined rocket on the launchpad, braced by the accompanying assemblage. McGreagor had used every means at his disposal, from liposuction to Botox, to maintain his lean-and-mean, youthful appearance, and now he strode around shaking the dark crown of his expertly woven hairpiece.

"This, ladies and gentlemen," McGreagor said, extending his hand toward the image, "is the future."

Hudson thought it looked like an insignificant Roman candle waiting to blow, in contrast to the bleak mesquite-covered hills and distant mountains. He continued to watch as his boss spoke about the upcoming planned launch to his movie star friends, rich investors and a small, select group of reporters. Several professional photographers scurried around unobtrusively, snapping pictures, while others panned back and forth with cameras mounted on tripods. It was McGreagor's show, and Hudson wondered which turned the rich son of a bitch on more, the spectacle or the actual thought of space travel.

"This is your chance, ladies and gentlemen," McGreagor continued, "to be part of the future. To make what we see in the movies a reality." He paused and milked the silence for all it was worth before adding, "You can get tickets for the first civilian, commercial trip into outer space, and have a time share in our fully inhabited station on the moon by the end of the decade."

A murmur of excitement snaked through the audience. Hudson watched and listened as the images changed on the big screen behind McGreagor, first showing the previously depicted rocket blasting off and coasting comfortably in orbit. The computer-generated image alternated for a while with shots of Earth obviously borrowed from one of the actual space shuttle flights, then the sleek rocket was shown reentering the atmosphere and landing on a desert airstrip with the ease of a descending 747.

"We're on track to have our first test flight in a few months," McGreagor said, moving to the edge of the stage as the screen behind him filled with more images of the spaceship maneuvering through the skies and landing again and again. "Our reentry technology is this close—" he held up his thumb and index finger an inch apart "—to being completed. Thanks to the efforts of two of the greatest scientific minds of the past and current centuries." He smiled and extended his arm toward the two older men, Terry Turner and Vassili Nabokovski, seated on the far side of the stage.

The audience applauded.

"This is your chance, ladies and gentlemen," McGreagor said on the tail end of the fading applause. "Your chance to be part of the greatest adventure of our era. Your chance to be part of the New International Independent Space Agency, NIISA."

More applause filled the auditorium.

The old son of a bitch has them eating out of the palm of his hand, Hudson thought. He's already got more money than the US Mint, and these rich bastards are going to be lining up to give him more. Hudson shook his head. Too bad it would soon be time to rain on this little parade. But any regrets he might have had were vastly overshadowed by the thoughts of how rich he himself was going to be. All he had to do was play his hand right, and make sure everything went according to the plan.

He pressed his left arm against his side, feeling the comforting reassurance of the Smith & Wesson M&P 40L. It was a bit bigger than he needed, but it was a mean-looking piece of steel and polymer. Hudson never knew when McGreagor would pull him aside, in one of his braggadocio moments, and urge Hudson to show one of the movie-star idiots what "a real weapon" looked like. Thus, the larger frame .40-caliber pistol was an appropriate choice.

Everything McGreagor did was based more on image and speculation than on results. And Hudson, as the chief of security, was expected to be part of the program, just like the two new rocket scientists his boss had recruited, Turner and Nabokovski. One American, one Russian, and both experts in the field of old ICBMs from another era, Turner from NASA and Nabokovski from the Soviet space program. If anyone could lick the puzzle of how to achieve a successful atmospheric reentry, it was those two. But Hudson knew the New International Independent Space Agency would never see the first civilian commercial space travel, much less build that station on the moon. Especially after Hudson made good on his delivery to the North Koreans: the proposed telemetry for NIISA's reentry system and two slightly worn nuclear physicists.

American Embassy
Culiacán, Sinaloa, Mexico

BOLAN AND GRIMALDI sat in the darkened room as the full-screen Skype image of Hal Brognola came into view. Seeing Brognola's scowling face as he set his ceramic mug on the desk before him let them know all was not well at Stony Man Farm.

"What's up?" Bolan asked. "Is your scowl a reflection on the results of the raid?"

"I just got off the phone with the White House."

"How'd that go?" Bolan asked.

Brognola sighed. "About as good as could be expected, considering the circumstances."

Bolan compressed his lips. More than just a few things about the ill-fated raid bothered him, but something indefinable danced through the inner recesses of his memory... Something out of place, but so far, he hadn't been able to put his finger on it.

"What about it, Striker? Is there any way to put lipstick on this pig?" the big Fed asked.

Instead of the mother lode they'd hoped for, they had recovered a small, rather disappointing amount of unprocessed coca plants and other drugs from the warehouse, and lost three Mexican marines, all good men, in the process.

"The drug seizure wasn't that impressive," Bolan said. "Which probably means that the full shipment was still being picked up and hadn't been deposited in the warehouse yet."

"It was bad intel from the get-go," Grimaldi said.

"What about the plane?" Brognola asked.

"It was destroyed," Bolan said. "Apparently, the guy who engaged me in the firefight dropped the grenade he was about to throw. It detonated and then set off the fuel tanks. The plane was a complete loss. They're going through the shell now. Preliminary reports showed five bodies inside. Six, if you include the grenadier."

"We recovered a briefcase loaded with American currency and euros," Grimaldi said. "Somebody was about to make a purchase."

"Which brings up the matter of our special prisoner," Brognola said. "The Cuban national. You got any idea what his angle is?"

"He's playing it close to his vest," Bolan said. "We'll know more once we can interrogate him."

"The Bureau's sending a pair of special agents down

there to do just that." Hal sat back in his chair and held his coffee mug in both hands. "I know that look, Striker. Is something else bothering you?"

"Somebody tipped them," he answered.

"You think they were tipped off in advance?"

"Not in advance," Bolan said. "Otherwise they would have set up an ambush. This was more like a last-minute notification. If they'd known we were coming, that plane wouldn't have landed, either." The events of the raid were running through his mind like a movie at double speed. The approach, the interdiction, the firefight… Then it hit him. Someone inside the warehouse had yelled that the marines had arrived, not the police. How did the person know it was the marines?

"I need to have a talk with Sergeant Martinez," Bolan said. "I think he's got a traitor in his group. Someone on the raid team tipped them as we were making the final approach."

Brognola raised his eyebrows. "That's not going to go over well with the administration, either here or in Mexico City. Do you have any hard proof?"

"Just a feeling," Bolan said.

"But when he gets a feeling," Grimaldi broke in, "you can pretty much take it to the bank."

"I don't know," Brognola said, shaking his head. "One of the reasons the marines were sent in was to prevent leaks to informants."

"This had to have been a last-minute tip-off. We were in close proximity up until the execution. Somebody must have had a cell phone and made a quick call, maybe contacting someone to call the compound and warn them."

Brognola heaved a sigh. "Okay, I'll pursue it from this end, too. See if Bear can pull some cell phone transmission records. So are you sure you can trust that Martinez guy?"

Bolan considered that, then nodded. "As sure as I can

be. He was right there alongside us when it all went down. And he was pretty upset about losing his men. You can't fake that kind of emotion."

Brognola nodded. "Keep me posted." His eyes narrowed. "Is there something else?"

"Another inconsistency. One of the hostiles down there, the guy from the plane who tried to take us out… I got a glimpse of his face before the grenade detonated. He looked Asian. Just thought I'd pass that along."

"Thanks. As I said, the FBI's sending a team to Mexico to interview the Cuban. I thought maybe you two could stick around and give them a hand."

"Give them a hand?" Grimaldi repeated with an exaggerated groan. "What does that mean?"

"See if the guy's legit, for one thing," Brognola said. "We know the Cubans have been working hand in hand with the cartels for years, smuggling drugs. With these new normalized relations with Havana, we're going to need all the intel we can gather to keep on top of things."

"We'll need a better cover," Bolan stated. "We were down here as 'civilian contractors' assisting the marines, remember?"

"I'll have your usual DOJ credentials flown down to the embassy tonight."

2

Tocumen International Airport
Panama City, Panama

Colonel Yi flipped shut the fake Chinese passport and
placed it into his pocket as he waited for his luggage to
clear customs. The rest of the Black Tiger team was going
through customs, as well. Yi directed one of his men to
take charge of the bags and strolled leisurely outside to
stand in the nighttime air. He scanned his surroundings,
looking for any possible foreign agents or police who might
be suspicious of an arriving group of Asians. Their passports listed them as Chinese, a Hong Kong acrobatic team,
which explained their elaborate equipment. And to the un-
trained eyes of the Panamanians, the distinctions between
Koreans and Chinese would be indistinguishable.

Seeing no telltale prying eyes, Yi removed a cigarette
pack from his pocket. He shook one out, placed it between
his lips and lit it as he moved to a position of modest seclu-
sion under a high concrete arch. Exhaling a cloud of smoke,
Yi casually took out his satellite phone and called Song.

"We have arrived in Panama," Yi said in Chinese, to maintain his team's cover.

"Did you encounter any problems?" General Song asked, also in Chinese.

"None so far. We are clearing customs and waiting for our local contact to pick us up. We will then obtain the rest of our equipment. Are the ships in position?"

"Their arrival is imminent." Song cleared his throat, which Yi knew was a bad sign. "However, there has been an unforeseen complication. The meeting in Mexico did not go well. Apparently, the Americans and some of their Mexican puppets interceded."

Yi considered that. "How much damage was done?"

"Sergeant Kwon acquitted himself most admirably, from what I've been told. He fought back gallantly and blew up the plane containing the others before the majority of the principles could be identified or captured."

"So the Iranians were not discovered?"

"Apparently not," Song said. "But the briefcase with the money was."

Yi knew that the Iranians had plenty of money to spend, so that was of little concern to him so long as the Americans did not link the money to Iran. It was, however, yet another reminder of the complexity of the plan—so many individual moving parts each dependent upon the other for the proper execution of purpose.

"Two prisoners were taken," Song said. "One is a simpleton guard, who has already been dealt with." He paused and exhaled loudly. "The other is one of the Cubans."

This information concerned Yi. He said nothing, awaiting further information.

"It seems," Song continued, "that this Cuban is withholding information at this time, so he can negotiate with the Americans. I have the information as to where he is being held. You must send the Black Dragon to silence him immediately."

Yi was not thrilled about sending his best man to effect an assassination in an unfamiliar land, but still, the Dragon had accomplished such difficult tasks before on foreign soil. Yi decided he would send a Black Tiger with the Dragon. It would impinge upon the operational effectiveness of his own assignment in Panama, but two men would assure success. While it wasn't certain how much the Cuban knew, or even if any early disclosure about the missiles would upset the delicate timetable, it was far better to leave nothing to chance.

"It will be done, sir," Yi said. "And what of Kim Soo-Han? All goes well with the American?"

The other man chuckled. "Of course. That part of the plan is my least concern."

Punta de las Sueños
Culiacán, Sinaloa, Mexico

JAMES HUDSON STOOD by the bed with the phone, watching the woman stroll around the room in her high heels and one of his white shirts, unbuttoned. The sight delighted him, even as he listened to the repetitive instructions from Dr. Phillip McGreagor over the cell phone.

"Remember," McGreagor said, "we're pulling out all the stops on this one. Besides employees, we'll be hosting investors of all sorts, most of whom are accustomed to having their every whim satisfied. Am I making myself clear?"

"Absolutely," Hudson said, watching as his companion plucked ice cubes from the plastic bucket and dropped them, one by one, into the two glasses.

"And make sure you've hired enough local police to

maintain security down there," McGreagor said. "We can't afford to have anything untoward happen."

The hotel was set on the beach, well away from the ramshackle houses of the nearby town. The beach and the grounds were patrolled by uniformed security carrying weapons. Hudson was sure of all this because he had already figured out a way to defeat all the measures. "I've gone over everything down here, sir," he said. "Believe me, it's tighter than a drum."

Hudson heard McGreagor sigh. "And have you made arrangements for the…entertainment? A couple of these high rollers have exotic tastes."

Exotic… The word fitted his companion to a T, he thought as she ambled back toward him, a glass of gin in each hand, the open front of the shirt giving him more than an eyeful of her stunning cleavage, her tight abdomen.

"Did you hear me?" McGreagor asked, his voice imbued with the customary irritation and truculence that set Hudson's teeth on edge.

"Yes, Doctor," Hudson said, figuring that the mention of the man's PhD would stroke his ego enough to lessen the customary chastisement.

"Well, then, say something, dammit. You know I hate it when you don't answer."

Hudson frowned as he accepted the drink, so angry at the long-distance criticism that he felt like throwing the glass against the wall. But he didn't. There would be time, later, to deal with this unctuous, demanding prick of a boss.

"I'll make sure the hookers are first-class," Hudson said.

"Dammit! Watch what you say. You never know who's listening."

"Sorry, sir." Hudson felt himself flush. McGreagor had a way of making him feel embarrassed and inadequate even if he was a couple thousand miles away.

"Use some common sense," McGreagor snapped.

"We've got to make this excursion flawless. If we're going to stay on schedule for our launch, we need to impress the shit out of these investors. We can't afford any slip-ups. Got it?"

"Yes, sir," Hudson said. "I got it."

"Good. Get everything set up and then get your ass back here."

Hudson ended the call and took a long gulp of the drink.

"Your boss is upset?" the woman asked, canting her head slightly.

He shook his head. "He's just being his typical, ass-hole self."

"So," she said, pulling Hudson close. "This will not interfere with our plans, will it?"

"No, no, of course not. Let's not worry about him. I can handle it."

"All is well, then?" she asked. "The company retreat will remain on schedule?"

"Everything's ducky, Kim Soo-Han," Hudson said, pronouncing each syllable of her name with delicious distinction. "Just ducky. Trust me."

Soon, he thought. Soon.

Café de Luca
Culiacán, Sinaloa, Mexico

BOLAN NODDED TO Martinez as the sergeant entered the small cantina and headed to their table. He'd changed into civilian clothes, as had Bolan and Grimaldi, but still hardly looked like a typical citizen out for an early-evening snack. He shook hands with the two Americans, sat, then shook his head.

"I have just come from telling the families of my fallen marines about the deaths of their loved ones. It was very sad."

Bolan nodded in commiseration. He knew the pain of loss.

The server arrived to take his order. Both Bolan and Grimaldi had bottles of beer on the table in front of them.

"Beer," Martinez said.

The woman left and the big marine leaned forward, his hefty forearms on the tabletop. "Now, what is it that you wished to speak to me about?"

"I've been thinking about the raid," Bolan said. "The men we lost. It shouldn't have gone down the way it did. We had the element of surprise."

Martinez compressed his lips and nodded, a look of anger in his dark eyes.

"Sí," he said. "I agree."

"Right before the firefight started, someone shouted and the lights and sirens began."

Martinez nodded again. "I remember."

"How did they discover we were there? They hadn't seen us, and we were moving up just like clockwork."

"What is it you are saying?"

"Someone on our team tipped them off during our approach. It's the only answer."

"No," Martinez said, shaking his head. "No. I will not believe this. I have fought and died beside my men. There is no possibility that one of them is a traitor."

"One of the cartel guards used the word *marines*," Bolan said. "He knew we were marines and not the police. How did he know that?"

Martinez looked down at the tabletop. Just as he was about to speak the server returned with his beer. She smiled at them as she set it down and asked if they needed anything else.

Bolan slipped her some pesos and shook his head. The woman smiled again and moved away.

"Think about it, Jesus," Grimaldi said. "I wasn't down

and dirty with you guys, but my partner's seldom wrong about such things."

The sergeant sat in silence for several seconds, not moving.

"You owe it to your men to check this out," Bolan said quietly.

Martinez slowly nodded.

"We can help you. We have resources we can use outside your agency. Outside the Mexican government."

Martinez twisted his lips into a scowl and looked directly into Bolan's eyes. "*Sí*, and if this is true, I will kill the traitor myself."

"We can worry about that when the time comes," Bolan said. "The first thing I need to stress is that you tell no one. I'm trusting you, but no one else at the moment."

Martinez nodded.

"Second," Bolan said, "I'll need the cell phone numbers of everyone involved, including any of the cartel's phone numbers on record."

Martinez nodded again. He removed his cell phone from the case on his belt and pressed a few numbers. "I will contact Captain Ruiz now, and obtain the information you request."

Bolan held up his hand and said, "Wait. I'd prefer to keep this just between us for the time being."

"But the captain—"

"Should only be informed if we are correct in our assumption," Bolan told him. "There's no reason to cast aspersions on good marines unless we're sure."

"Of course," Martinez said, and held his phone toward the Executioner.

Bolan shook his head and smiled fractionally. "I don't want yours."

"Take it anyway," Martinez said. "I would never ask

or expect my men to do something that I am not willing to do, as well."

Bolan again declined the offer. Before he could say anything more, Martinez's cell phone flashed and vibrated, signaling an incoming call. He glanced at the number on the screen, his brow furrowing, and answered it.

The Executioner followed the one-sided conversation as best he could. It seemed to contain disconcerting news. Martinez issued a couple of directives, terminated the call and replaced the cell in his belt case.

"One of the prisoners is dead," he said. "The cartel guard. He was found strangled in his cell. I was told he hanged himself."

"What about the Cuban?" Bolan asked.

"I gave orders that he be guarded around the clock. Your government is sending agents to conduct an interrogation, right?"

"Right. We're heading over to the airport in a little while to pick them up. It's imperative that nothing happens to the Cuban. We need to interview him," Bolan stated.

Martinez stood, his face set with a grim expression. "I will go to the jail now and personally see to it."

Bolan and Grimaldi rose in turn, and the Executioner extended his hand. "We appreciate your help."

As they shook hands, Martinez's expression did not waver. "And I appreciate yours. If there is a traitor in our midst, we must find him swiftly."

Abandoned warehouse
Panama City, Panama

YI WATCHED AS the Black Tiger squad went through the various inspections of the weapons the cartel agent had brought. Even though the warehouse was deserted and empty, the lights worked fine. The gangsters had set up a series of flimsy folding tables at various points around the room for the weapons assembly. The guns glistened with oil as the team fieldstripped them, wiped them down and reassembled them with practiced ease. The weapons were all Western and American brands, M-16 rifles, Glock handguns, some Heckler & Koch submachine guns, but that did not matter. His Black Tigers had been trained on all weapons and were very familiar with these. Yi put aside his personal preference for his weapons of choice, the Chinese-made AK-47 and the 9 mm Baek Du San pistol, and smacked the fully loaded magazine into the Glock 17. He inserted the pistol into the low-slug tactical holster on his right thigh and slipped the sound suppressor into his pants pocket. He was a bit dissatisfied with the suppressor. The cylindrical attachment was so large that, once attached to the barrel of the weapon, the cam prevented proper sight alignment. However, the Western weapons would have to suffice for the time being.

The two men, one Mexican and the other Panamanian, who had brought the weapons stood off to the side and watched, each with a smirking expression on his face. The Mexican's cream-colored sport jacket looked as if it needed cleaning. Half-moons of sweat had soaked through the underarms. Yi could relate. The heat and humidity in this place were so oppressive it was like standing fully clothed in a steam bath.

The gangster from Panama was more sensibly dressed, wearing a loose chambray shirt with the sleeves razored off. He was smaller than the Mexican, but no less unctuous.

"How you like them babies, huh?" he said.

Yi stared at him and replied, "They are far from ideal, but they will suit our purpose. Is there any word from your other men?"

"The ones that went north with yours?" the Panamanian asked. He smiled. "I'm sure they are there by now."

"I wish you to verify that," Yi said. "I need to report to my superiors."

The two gangsters exchanged glances and smirked again.

Yi's dislike of these men grew, and he considered his options. At this point, he still needed their cooperation, to a degree, so striking down one or both of them might not yet be appropriate. But still, experience had taught him to have little tolerance for disrespect. It could undermine operational effectiveness as quickly as poor planning.

"I think we need to report to ours, as well," the Mexican said. "And we need to see the money."

Yi stared at them for a few seconds, then gestured for the Iranian, Basir Farrokhzad, to approach. The man strode forward and set the briefcase on the small card table. As his hands moved to the twin safety catches, Yi stepped between the two gangsters and held his right hand above the briefcase. "No."

The two gangsters looked at him.

"What you mean, no?" the Mexican snarled. "We gotta see the money now."

"You see the money," Yi said, "after you have verified that the Black Dragon and Corporal Wang have arrived at their destination. I want a progress report."

"The Black Dragon," the Panamanian gangster said with a laugh. He put his index fingers next to his eyelids and pulled them back, narrowing his gaze. "Does he breathe fire, like Godzilla?"

"It would be wise for you to show me the proper respect," Yi said.

"Listen, you little prick," the Mexican said, his finger poking at Yi's chest. "You're in our house now. You do like we say, or it could get bad for you."

Yi kept his hand hovering above the briefcase. Farrokhzad looked nervous.

"Make the call to verify," Yi said. "Then you can count your money."

The Mexican and Panamanian exchanged glances and a laugh.

The Mexican muttered something Yi took to be a vulgarity, and reached inside his cream-colored jacket. As he started to withdraw a semiautomatic pistol, Yi shifted his weight, using his left hand to seize the Mexican's gun hand in a grip of steel, while the palm of his right smashed into the other man's nose. He pulled the gangster's arm outward and then chopped his extended elbow with a knife hand blow. The Mexican screamed in pain as Yi stripped the gun from his fingers.

A switchblade knife clicked open in the Panamanian's right hand, but Yi pivoted, bringing his right foot upward, delivering a quick and powerful crescent kick and knocking the Panamanian's hand away. Yi's left hand chopped his adversary's wrist, causing the knife to drop to the floor. The man grunted in pain as Yi's foot whipped upward with a hooking back kick, connecting with the rear of the gangster's head. His eyes rolled upward and he crumpled to the floor. Yi pivoted again, this time delivering a roundhouse kick to the Mexican's face, and he collapsed, as well. The colonel bent to retrieve the knife, hefting it in his hand to consider the balance and weight.

The Mexican rolled onto his back, glaring up at Yi. The colonel's arm cocked back and thrust forward with a blur. Seconds later, the knife vibrated, stuck in the wooden floor a few inches from the Mexican's groin. The gangster's face sagged.

"As I told you, show proper respect," Yi said in a low, guttural voice. "Now make the call." He racked back the slide on the Mexican's weapon, a flashy chrome Beretta 92F, ejecting the round in the chamber. Yi then dropped the magazine and hurled it toward the far wall of the warehouse. He then gripped the barrel and disassembled the pistol, flinging the parts in different directions. "Then you may count your money."

The Mexican nodded, took out his cell phone and hastily scrolled through the numbers. His lips twisted into a quick, nervous smile and he nodded, a look of fear in his eyes. Yi knew he would have no more trouble with this man.

The colonel allowed himself to be imbued with a slight sense of satisfaction as he glanced at the other gangster, who was still unconscious on the floor. It had been some time since he had taken out an adversary with a single kick. It was good to know that his practice had kept him sharp.

Force, and the judicious use of it, Yi thought, always commanded respect.

The vision of one of the great Yi Sun-Shin's all-powerful armored dragon ships coursing through the ocean waters in ages past flashed in his mind's eye.

Force, he thought. The universal language.

Culiacán International Airport
Culiacán, Sinaloa, Mexico

BOLAN AND GRIMALDI waited in the long hallway outside the international arrivals section. At the American Embassy they had been given brief descriptions of what the two FBI agents looked like, one Asian male, one Hispanic female, as well as photos. The male, Henry Chong, was Korean-American, and fluent in several languages including Korean, Chinese, Spanish, Farsi and Arabic. The female, Teresa Stevenson, was of Cuban descent and fluent in a host of languages, as well.

As they stood watching and waiting for the two federal agents, Bolan mentally reviewed the case. A lot would depend on what the Cuban prisoner had to say. If he could corroborate that the cartel guards had been tipped off just prior to the raid, it might help the Executioner ferret out the traitor.

No one seemed to be moving on the other side of the glass partition where the customs agents waited for incoming arrivals.

"I'm going to check in with Hal," Bolan said, taking out his sat phone.

He strolled through the series of glass doors and watched the flow of people entering and exiting the airport. A line of taxis waited off to the left. Behind him, far out on the runways, Bolan could hear the revving of a powerful jet engine getting ready for takeoff. He stood by one of the round concrete pillars, took one last look around the area as he raised the sat phone and punched in the number of Brognola's direct line.

The big Fed answered on the first ring. "I figured you'd call," he said. "Have Chong and Stevenson shown up yet?"

"We're still waiting."

"Aaron's been checking into those cell phone numbers you gave us and comparing them to recorded calls we've been able to pinpoint in the area. There's the number of a burner phone that called one of the cartel's cells shortly before you guys hit them, if we've got the timing right. Then the cartel phone called one of the guys at the warehouse."

Bolan knew the chances of identifying someone from the number of a disposable cell phone was nearly impossible, even for an expert as adept at hacking as Aaron "the Bear" Kurtzman.

"Where was it purchased?"

Brognola uttered a short, hard laugh. "Mexico City. So that narrows your suspect list down to what, around twenty million?"

"Did the Bear find anything else?"

"Whoever was using the burner was in regular contact with the cartel. The number's still in use. In fact, we found a few more calls took place earlier today, to guess what?" Brognola waited a beat and then said, "A couple more burner phones, one purchased in Mexico City, and the other one in Hong Kong."

"That fits with the Asian connection," Bolan said. He glanced at his watch. "You said the FBI agents' flight was supposed to land at 1925?"

"Roger that."

It was now 1930. "Well, they should be clearing customs soon. I'd better get back."

Brognola told him to stay safe.

"Will do," Bolan said. "And, Hal, email those burner phone numbers when you get a chance."

Bolan ended the call and rejoined Grimaldi by the exits, watching as a new throng of people began moving through the doors. The Executioner kept scanning the crowd and caught a glimpse of a familiar face. He moved on an intercept course and stepped in front of Captain Ruiz and another man.

Ruiz blinked in surprise, then seemed to recognize Bolan. The other man, small and slightly built, wearing a blue suit and glasses, smiled under a bushy mustache and said in Spanish, "Excuse us, sir, but we are in a hurry."

"Sí," Bolan said, adding in English, "I just wanted to say hello to Captain Ruiz."

Ruiz spoke rapidly to the other man in Spanish, then added in halting English, "These are…American agents who assisted on raid against cartel."

The bespectacled man smiled and nodded. "Ah, you are American? The captain tells me you are very brave men. You are meeting some friends here, no?"

Bolan and Grimaldi nodded.

"Bueno. We are meeting some people as well, but perhaps we can assist you," the man said. "Captain Ruiz brought me along to act as his official translator."

"The people you're meeting are from the United States?" Bolan asked.

"What?" the bespectacled man said, then turned to Ruiz and fired off a quick sentence in Spanish.

Ruiz smiled and shook his head. His companion turned back to Bolan and Grimaldi and smiled in turn. "I am sorry, but it is a private matter. It has to do with his family."

Bolan nodded and said, "I understand. By the way, I heard that one of the prisoners we took on the raid was killed."

Again the bespectacled man did a rapid-fire translation, after which Ruiz nodded, lifting an eyebrow and giving a sigh of regret. "Very bad thing."

"We have made arrangements," the shorter man said, "to safeguard the remaining prisoner so that nothing unfortunate happens to him. He has been placed in a secure location."

"I appreciate that," Bolan said. He glanced at Ruiz, who seemed calm. "Captain, I know I can speak for my friend when I say that we look forward to our next meeting."

Ruiz nodded and smiled. "Thank you very much."

Beyond them, Chong and Stevenson walked through the customs' doors, each pulling a small carry-on.

"Looks like our friends are here now," Grimaldi stated.

The bespectacled man whispered something to Ruiz, who turned toward the approaching special agents. "Welcome to Mexico," he said in English, punctuating it with a wide smile.

Stevenson replied in Spanish, as did Chong. Ruiz raised his eyebrows, and mumbled something to the bespectacled man, who then said, "The captain is impressed that you speak our language so well. He hopes you both have a fortuitous stay in our country."

Ruiz held out a card bearing his name, title and cell phone number. Bolan took it with a nod of thanks.

"Please let us know," the translator said, "if there is any way we can be of further assistance."

"We certainly will," Grimaldi replied jovially.

The captain and his assistant walked off in the direction of domestic arrivals.

"I'm Henry Chong. You must be Matt Cooper and Jack White," the agent said, extending his hand toward Bolan, then Grimaldi. Chong nodded toward Ruiz and the other man. "Looks like a friendly bunch down here."

"Looks like," Bolan said. He turned to the female agent. "Welcome to Mexico, Agent Stevenson."

She smiled and shook his hand.

Grimaldi thrust his hand toward Stevenson in turn. "I second that. Anything you need, just ask ole Jack."

"Let's get out of here," Bolan suggested. "Time's wasting."

3

National Police Warehouse Number 7
Panama Canal Zone

From their vantage point within the dense forest, the industrial center spread out before them like a lit-up shopping mall. The trees and shrubbery had been cleared for approximately thirty meters around the warehouses, and a metal fence surrounded the compound, topped by concertina wire.

These were pathetic safeguards. The task seemed almost too easy, and Yi did not want his men to be lulled into a false sense of security. Eventually, they were bound to meet stiffer resistance, but a wise man gratefully accepted good fortune when it was presented to him.

Yi ordered Lieutenant Yoon to have the Black Tigers spread out and remain undercover while the scouts cut through the fence and reconnoitered. He then turned to the Panamanian gangster, who was bound with his hands behind his back. The Mexican, also bound, was next to him. After the confrontation at the warehouse during the acquisition of the weapons, Yi felt it was prudent not to trust either man any longer, and to treat them as captured collaborators.

"Which building houses the missiles?" Yi asked in English.

The Panamanian, whose lips were torn and bloody, blinked in the darkness. "I told you, number seven."

Yi needed to confirm that the other elements of the plan were in place. As he took out his cell phone, the Panamanian asked, "You gonna let us go now?"

Yi paused and stared at the man. Being on foreign soil, he still needed a modicum of cooperation from these charlatans, but knew he couldn't trust either of them. But it would not serve his purposes to let them know that neither had much longer to live. Instead, he nodded, and said, "If you have told me the truth, I will set you both free once this phase of the mission has been completed."

The Mexican groaned. "Let us go now. We can help you, amigo."

"Sí," the Panamanian added. "We are *mucho* sorry for the problem before. We just like to have a little fun, that's all."

Yi ignored the pleas and speed-dialed a number on his cell phone. It rang only once before a voice answered.

The colonel spoke in Korean, knowing that neither the Mexican nor the Panamanian would be able to follow the conversation. "We are ready at the target. Are your men ready with the transportation?"

"Yes. We are standing by at the designated point."

Yi disconnected. The trucks were there. They needed only to retake the missiles now.

He thought about the captured Cuban. Without knowing if the man had talked, or how much he had divulged about the ongoing plan, it was impossible to judge their chances for complete success. Still, what did the Cuban really know? He knew about the missiles, and he knew which foreign powers were involved in the transaction. With that information in their hands, the Americans could surmise that the reacquisition of the missiles was a possibility. Eventually, this fact would become obvious to all involved, but the timing of this revelation was critical. It would not do to have the enemy alerted too soon about the involvement of the Iranians. Thus, it was better that this Cuban loose end be tied up quickly.

Yi called the Black Dragon, who answered after the first ring.

"What is your status?" Yi asked.

"We have left the airport and are en route to the location," the Black Dragon said. "We have met with our contact here, and he has supplied the necessary information and equipment. We should have the assignment completed shortly."

"Very well," Yi said. "Once you have accomplished the task, proceed to the next rendezvous point. We will meet you there."

After hearing the acknowledgment, Yi disconnected. He had immense trust in the Dragon's ability to carry out the delegated assignment successfully. It was now time to complete this phase.

Yi checked with the scouts, who reported only two sentries guarding the building. Ordinarily, Yi would have ordered the scouts to tactically neutralize them, but doing so in this instance would have international repercussions. It was one thing to kill a few puppet soldiers from South Korea, or even some Americans in the DMZ, but killing two Panamanian nationals in their own land could adversely affect his country's future usage of the canal. Retaking the missiles could be labeled "a recovery of illegally seized property," even though they had been originally seized due to the UN charter prohibiting sale of weaponry to his country. The legitimacy of such a decree could always be disputed and ignored.

"Scouts, neutralize the sentries as previously directed," Yi said into his radio. "Perimeter men, prepare the breaches in the fence line."

He lifted the night-vision binoculars and watched as the two scouts approached the Panamanian sentries, while other Black Tigers crawled to the fence with the cutting instruments. Both guards were standing casually, smoking, their weapons slung haphazardly on their shoulders.

The first Black Tiger crept closer to the sentries, one of whom seemed to notice something moving toward them. The approaching Black Tiger began a quick sprint, covering the distance between them in scant seconds. He leaped into the air and delivered a quick flying kick to the back of the nearer man. The cigarette tumbled from the other sentry's mouth as he tried to unsling his weapon, but the Black Tiger landed in a fighting stance and incapacitated him with a few deft blows.

Yi scanned the rest of the area. Three of his men had moved forward to cut entry points through the chain-link fence. They stood by in silent readiness, signaling that their tasks had been completed. Yi ordered the remainder of his team to move in and secure the warehouse. He watched through the night-vision goggles as the other Black Tigers ran across the clearing as the men at the fence peeled back the metal squares in synchronous fashion.

The Tigers descended upon the warehouse, and within ninety seconds the team leader advised that the building was secure. Yi ordered the Panamanian sentries to be brought inside, and then switched his radio frequency to that of the convoy.

"We have secured the facility," he said. "You may now enter."

"Yes, sir!"

Yi allowed himself a slight smile. This part of the mission had gone off without a hitch. He could not help but wonder how the Black Dragon was faring farther north, in Mexico.

La Palacio de Oro Hotel
Culiacán, Sinaloa, Mexico

THE HOTEL SUITE was spacious and well furnished. In the anteroom beyond the bedroom, two Mexican marines with MP-5s stood guard by the door, and Sergeant Martinez sat in a chair opposite Bolan and Grimaldi. They watched and listened as Special Agents Chong and Stevenson interviewed the Cuban, who had identified himself as Raul Espinoza. He had told them about his presence in the country and his connection to the Mexican cartel. Even though Espinoza had laid things out in a straightforward manner, admitting he was a frequent participant in moving drugs from South America through Cuba and into Mexico, it was obvious that he was holding something back. The Cuban had hinted at having something very significant to trade, but remained coy.

"Gimme a deal in writing," Espinoza demanded. "Then I'll tell you what you wanna know."

Both special agents looked frustrated. Bolan wanted to take a crack at the interrogation, but he remained passive. This was the FBI's show, and he had to let them run it, at least for the short term.

"Gimme a cigarette," Espinoza said. "And what about some room service?"

Grimaldi volunteered to go get a pack and headed for the door.

"Make it a big cigar instead," Espinoza said. "A *cubano*, if you can find one."

Grimaldi stepped next to one of the marines, opened the

door a crack, looked down the hallway and then quickly slipped out.

"Let's get back to business," Stevenson said.

Espinoza leaned back in the soft easy chair and looked at Martinez. "Hey, *jefe*, can you get someone to make me some Cuban-style beans and rice?"

Martinez remained silent, shooting him a hard stare.

Bolan knew the loss of the three marines was weighing heavily on the man. He put a hand on Martinez's shoulder. "Don't let him get to you."

Martinez took in a deep breath, his mouth twisting into a scowl, and exhaled loudly. "*Sí*, I know. He is a pig, but a useful pig." He stood and headed for the door.

Bolan stood, too.

"Hey, *jefe*!" Espinoza called out. "You gonna go see 'bout my food?"

Chong's head whipped around and he held up his hand. "No food until we finish this interview."

"Relax," Bolan said. "We just need some air."

They went to the door and Martinez opened it a crack, repeating Grimaldi's pattern, and then both men slipped into the hallway.

As they walked to the elevators, Martinez shook his head. "I wish we could have a crack at him," he said. "Those two…" He shook his head. "They are very inexperienced."

Bolan nodded and took out his sat phone. "Let me see if my friends were able to turn up anything regarding that other matter we talked about."

Martinez nodded and pushed the button for the elevator. "Let us go up to the roof. The reception will be better."

The elevator doors opened and they both stepped in. They were on the sixth floor, and Martinez pressed the button for the twelfth. After riding up in silence to the top floor, they headed for the stairway that led to the roof.

Something ground under the sole of Bolan's boot in the stairwell. He glanced down and saw it was a tiny stone.

As they made their way onto the roof, their boots made crunching noises. The Executioner did a quick scan, noting that the tarred surface was covered with fine stones. The stone in the stairway indicated that someone had visited this area. Seeing no one, Bolan scanned the roof again and saw two sets of ropes wrapped around the crenulated edge of the building, on the same side as the room in which they'd been conducting the interrogation. He strode over to check and saw an empty window-washing scaffold suspended about ten feet below. One of the tied-off ropes appeared to be thin nylon, designed more for rappelling than as a safety line. Still, the positioning of the scaffold was at least fifteen feet to the right of the room where they were holding the Cuban.

Bolan turned back to Martinez. "Are we certain this location is secure?" he asked.

The sergeant shrugged. "Captain Ruiz assured me that it was. Why?"

Bolan shook his head and pressed the speed dial on his sat phone to contact Brognola, who was a continent away. He answered with his customary quickness.

"How's the interrogation going?" he asked.

"Nothing yet," Bolan said. "The two FBI agents they sent down here are long on enthusiasm, but short on experience."

"Figures," Brognola replied. "Aaron's been slashing and hacking into all sorts of phone records for the region in question. He's come up with zilch regarding named accounts. He's still digging for more about that one particular burner phone that repeatedly called the number linked to the cartel. What time, exactly, did your raid go down?"

"At 0315."

"Hmm," Brognola said, "this is interesting. At 0315,

records show a burner phone calling another burner, a known cartel number, that in turn called another burner, with that signal pinging off a remote tower in the vicinity of the compound. The call only lasted twelve seconds. The cartel burner phone then called one of the numbers that we've matched to the confiscated cell phones you guys found in the compound. Like someone was relaying a message."

"That would fit," Bolan said. "Whoever made that first call had to do so surreptitiously, and probably didn't have the number to directly call the guards in the compound. So he called his regular cartel contact, and had him relay the news that the marines had landed. Email me that burner number, will you?"

"Yeah, sorry about that," Brognola said. "There you go. You need anything else?"

"I'll advise," Bolan said, and terminated the call. His second cell phone, the one he used to communicate with Grimaldi, was vibrating.

Bolan answered it and heard his partner say, "I'm back, and the Feds want to talk to you and Martinez. Right away."

"They catch a break?" Bolan asked.

"Maybe," Grimaldi said. "It looks like they let this turkey order room service."

"We're on our way."

He and Martinez pulled open the door and trotted down the stairwell. As they stood waiting for the elevator, the big Mexican marine leaned close to Bolan and spoke in a low tone. "If one of my men is a traitor, I will cut out his heart and feed it to the dogs in the street."

Bolan nodded.

After taking the elevator, the two proceeded down the hallway to the room. Martinez knocked on the door in a specific pattern, and it opened a crack. An eye appeared and then the door swung wider. Bolan saw Grimaldi standing in the room talking with Stevenson and Chong as Espinoza, grinning, stood near a linen-covered cart. The waiter had removed the covers from several dishes and placed the serving spoons. A bottle of champagne rested in a metal container of ice. The waiter pushed the cart toward the bedroom.

"Hey, amigos," Espinoza said. "This is more like it. I want this kind of service all the way to Miami. And see if you can get me a couple of pretty women." He emitted a guttural laugh as he looked directly at Stevenson and added, "Unless you want to join me, sweetie."

Stevenson's face flushed and her eyes shot toward Bolan and the others. She turned to the Cuban and said, "Go into the other room so I don't have to smell you or your stinky cigar."

Espinoza smirked and said, "Okay, bitch."

"Hey, asshole," Grimaldi said. "Watch your mouth."

Espinoza laughed again and followed the waiter into the bedroom.

"The Cuban give you anything?" Bolan asked.

"Plenty," Chong said. His face held a look of excitement. "He says that—"

Martinez held up his hand. "Perhaps we should step into the hallway." He glanced at Bolan, who nodded.

Chong appeared slightly confused, but he and Stevenson followed Bolan, Grimaldi and Martinez through the doorway. Martinez closed the door behind them.

"My apologies," the sergeant said, "but we have some concerns about possible corruption among my men."

Chong nodded, the excitement fading from his face. "Okay, duly noted. We'll be taking Espinoza off your hands immediately. We've got to get him someplace to complete this interrogation."

"What did he say?" Bolan asked.

"Something big," Chong said. "Unbelievably big."

Bolan raised his eyebrows questioningly. "You care to share it with us?"

Chong and Stevenson looked at each other. Finally, Chong nodded and said, "Okay, but first we'll have to check with our supervisor. I don't need to remind you that this is a Bureau case. So I don't appreciate interference in our interrogation."

"What are you talking about?" Bolan asked.

"I specifically told you no food until we were ready," the agent said. "Why did you override that and order room service?"

"We didn't," Bolan said.

A sudden muffled, clinking sound, followed by a grunt, emanated from behind the closed door.

Bolan and Grimaldi exchanged glances, then the Executioner unleathered his pistol. Martinez moved to the door and began the systematic series of knocks to gain entry.

No response.

Martinez stepped back, lifted his leg and kicked the area under the locking assembly. The door stayed in place. The sergeant was about to deliver another kick when the sound of automatic gunfire erupted inside the suite.

Bolan pushed Martinez to the side. More gunfire sounded, and a row of bulges buckled the top of the door. Grimaldi stood back and mule-kicked the bottom of the door, causing it to swing inward. Bolan, his weapon held at combat ready, hurtled through the opening, stepping over the bodies of two fallen marines. Both men lay on the floor amid liquid stains, shards of shattered glass and the jagged remnants of a broken champagne bottle. Their eyes were glazed and sightless, and a trail of blood spilled from one man's throat.

The door separating the anteroom from the bedroom was closed. Bolan did a combat sweep of the entire room in a few seconds, then moved to the short, narrow hall-way that led to the bedroom. That door was locked, too. The Executioner stepped back and delivered a powerful kick just below the doorknob. This door, which was thin-ner and less fortified than the other one, flew open and smacked against the wall. Bolan entered this room and did another sweep.

Espinoza lay facedown in the middle of the floor, be-tween the bed and the portable dinner cart.

The window was open and the white jacket that the waiter had been wearing was on the floor. As Grimaldi entered the room, his SIG Sauer extended, Bolan motioned for him to check Espinoza. The Executioner moved to the open window and took a quick look, seeing a man in dark clothing rappelling down the side of the building with ac-complished ease. Bolan hesitated, unsure of the figure's identity or status. The last thing he wanted to do was to shoot one of Martinez's men.

In the alley below flashes of gunfire appeared.

Automatic weapons.

Bolan knew the marines guarding the perimeter had MP-5s. He gave another quick glance downward and saw a man returning fire, the flashes and sound obviously subdued by a suppressor. The man in black completed his rappel. He and the second man jumped into a waiting vehicle—some sort of van—which took off down the alley and screeched around the corner.

Martinez, screaming instructions into his radio to his perimeter men, entered the room, followed by Chong and Stevenson, both of whom appeared to be in a state of shock or disbelief.

Bolan looked at Grimaldi, who was kneeling by Espi-noza. The Stony Man pilot shook his head.

National Police Warehouse Number 7
Panama Canal Zone

YI WATCHED WITH satisfaction as the final truck pulled out of the warehouse and started the journey to the coast. The Panamanians hadn't even moved the missiles from the flat-bed trailers, no doubt anticipating that the United Nations, which had ordered the seizure months ago, would soon be reclaiming them. But thankfully, the organization moved slowly under the guise of adherence to what they called "international law."

What nonsense, Yi thought.

All that was needed to achieve the reacquisition had been to detach the empty flatbeds of the trucks that they'd brought and attach those carrying the missiles. It had ex-pedited the mission significantly. The missiles had been covered by tarps so as not to be visible. Yi hadn't even needed the truck bearing the crane that had been acquired prior to their arrival. And best of all, they couldn't even be accused of stealing the trailers, since they were leaving the empty ones in their place. All that remained was to es-cort his country's rightful property to the coast and see to it that the missiles were expeditiously placed on the ship.

Yoon approached him. "What are your orders regard-ing the prisoners, sir?"

"Be certain that the men guarding this compound are not harmed," Yi said. "Tie them securely and find a place to confine them. The others we bring with us."

The lieutenant barked an affirmation, then turned away to carry out the order.

Yi watched as Yoon directed three of the men to take the two Panamanian guards into the back office area of the building. They would no doubt be discovered in the morning, when the shift would rotate, but by that time the missiles would be aboard the ship and in international waters, en route to the homeland.

Yi's cell phone vibrated in his pocket. He retrieved it, glanced at the screen and answered.

"It has been done," the Black Dragon said.

"Any complications?"

"I was not able to question him."

Yi considered that. It would have been useful to know exactly what the Cuban had told the Americans, but at this point it was unimportant. Eventual discovery was not only inevitable, but it was also desirable, at the appropriate juncture. He would have to proceed on the assumption that their presence was now known, which meant that speed in the movement of the missiles was of the essence.

"Any other problems?" Yi asked.

"None."

"Very well," Yi said. "Proceed to the next location and await my arrival."

After hearing an acknowledgment, Yi terminated the call. He keyed his radio mic and advised all the Black Tigers to assemble at their transport vehicles. They were ahead of schedule, which was good, but there was no time to dally. All that remained was to escort the missiles to the coast, supervise the loading procedure and catch his plane for the Mexican resort.

Two of his men marched the Panamanian and Mexican gangsters past him, toward the trucks. He needed the Mexican to assure a few more details, but the other one's usefulness had expired. Yi barked an order to place the prisoners in separate vehicles. He could dispose of the Panamanian on the way and leave the body in some wooded area. Or he could order both men to be taken on the ship and dumped at sea. Either way, the two gangsters were little more than excess trash at this point, loose ends that would be tied.

La Palacio de Oro Hotel
Culiacán, Sinaloa, Mexico

BOLAN WATCHED MARTINEZ make the sign of the cross as his two marines were removed from the hotel suite. Captain Ruiz and his bespectacled translator, Senor Vargas, stood by with sour looks on their faces. Grimaldi stood off to the side with Stevenson and Chong.

"The captain demands to know how this occurred," Vargas said.

Bolan noticed tears glistening in Martinez's eyes.

It had been a setup from the inside, that was for sure, but the Executioner knew Martinez wasn't involved. There was no way to fake his emotional response.

"Your two marines were by the door," Bolan said. "Right where they were supposed to be." He stepped to the center of the floor, next to the bloodstain on the carpet. "This broken glass is obviously from that." He pointed to the fractured champagne bottle. "The most likely scenario is the assassin came disguised as the waiter."

Vargas relayed this to Ruiz, who muttered something inaudible.

"Sergeant, you didn't check him?" Vargas yelled at Martinez.

"Hey, we checked him," Grimaldi replied. "I looked under the plate covers, and your marines patted the guy down and wanded him with the metal detector."

"Obviously," Vargas said with a sneer, "your efforts were substandard. Three men are dead."

Agents Stevenson and Chong seemed lost in the dynamics of the situation.

Grimaldi stood taller and seemed ready to respond until Bolan shot him a look.

"Yeah, whatever," the pilot said, and shrugged.

"Actually," Bolan continued, "the waiter was a trained

assassin who didn't need a weapon." He paused and waited for their eyes to fall on him once again. "He's highly skilled in the martial arts."

"And you know this how?" Vargas asked.

Bolan pointed to the other room and then the broken bottle. "Once he'd been frisked and the serving tray had been checked, the waiter rolled it into the bedroom, followed by the Cuban. If you remember, the magnum of champagne was in an ice bucket."

The others nodded in agreement.

"Once in the bedroom, and out of sight of the marines," Bolan said, "he most likely incapacitated Espinoza with a martial arts blow. He then removed the champagne bottle and returned to the two marines." The Executioner pointed to the bloody carpeting again. "He approached them, most likely with some pretext to get them off guard, and hit one cross the face with the bottle, causing it to shatter. The assassin then used the broken bottle to slash the other man's throat. He must have heard us trying to gain access, and went back into the bedroom." Bolan walked through the door and into the next room, where he stopped. The others followed.

"After closing and locking this door," he continued, "the assassin finished off Espinoza, figuring we were only seconds away from gaining entry." The Executioner looked at Vargas, who was translating his speech for Ruiz. "He then dropped his waiter's jacket there—" Bolan pointed to the garment on the floor "—and went to the window, signaling a confederate down below. As we now know, this was at least a two-man operation."

Ruiz muttered something to Vargas.

"But how did he descend from this height?" Vargas asked. "We are six stories up."

"There's a window washer's scaffold parked up top on this side of the building," Bolan said. "He went up there earlier and tied off his rappelling rope next to it. That line was long enough to reach the ground, and his partner in the alley simply walked it over to the appropriate window. The assassin hooked up here." Bolan patted the window-sill. "Then he rappelled down, swinging over to use the scaffold as cover from above. That's when your perimeter men tried to intercede, and the firefight started."

"Three more dead *marinas*," Vargas said to Martinez, his face a mask of contempt. "Plus the two up here. This has been a fiasco, brought about by your incompetence."

Martinez frowned, looking physically drained. "You will have my resignation in the morning," he said to Ruiz in Spanish.

Bolan took out his sat phone and pressed some numbers. He stopped and looked at the group. "Maybe we should review what we know and what we don't know. First, we're sure that the assassin was highly skilled in the martial arts, capable of killing three men while he himself was unharmed." He pressed another sequence of numbers, scanned the screen and nodded slightly. "Second, we know that the assassin knew exactly where we were holding Espinoza, and had time to put his escape plan in place."

Bolan looked at Martinez. "Remember that stone we found in the stairwell to the roof? Somebody was up there before we were. The stone probably came from the assassin's shoe."

Martinez nodded, his mouth compressing into a resolute line.

"And how did the assassin not only know that we had Espinoza in this hotel, but also the exact room number?" Bolan pressed the call button and then held the phone to his ear. "Obviously, somebody tipped him off." He waited a few beats, then added, "It's ringing."

The room was silent, except for a slight trickle of sound—the vibration of a cell phone.

Ruiz reached into his pants pocket. The vibrating noise ceased.

"¿Qué pasa?" he asked.

"My associates obtained the number of the burner phone that was used to tip off the cartel guards," Bolan said. "I just called it."

The captain's eyes widened, darting from Bolan to Martinez, and then back to Bolan.

"No, no," Ruiz said. *"No es possible. No es mio."*

Martinez grabbed Ruiz by the throat and began to strangle him. *"¡Hijo de puta!"*

As he was being bent over backward, Ruiz tried to break Martinez's grip. His hands reached under his loose-fitting shirt and came up with a pistol that he pressed into Martinez's stomach.

Bolan grabbed the weapon and tore it away from Martinez's abdomen just as the flash of the blast seared past the big man's shirt. With a deft move, Bolan twisted the pistol from Ruiz's hand, and then grabbed Martinez's left wrist.

"Let him go, amigo," the soldier said. "He's not worth it."

"He killed my men," Martinez gritted through clenched teeth.

"I know," Bolan said, "but don't lower yourself to his level. You're a man of honor. *Eres un marina.*"

Martinez slowly loosened his grip on Ruiz, who sank to the floor.

Bolan still had his hand on Martinez's arm.

Vargas glanced at Martinez, turned and started to run for the door.

"Jack," Bolan said.

Grimaldi pivoted and delivered a solid left hook into Vargas's gut. The bespectacled translator sank to his knees.

Private Air Field, NIISA Headquarters
Adobe Flats, New Mexico

BRIGHT LIGHTS ILLUMINATED the area outside the hangar. James Hudson watched as the luggage for all the investor guests and employees was loaded on board the aircraft. He knew that McGreagor would still be partying with everyone inside the hangar. The billionaire would be showing off his latest acquisitions, former NASA engineer Terry Turner and Russian nuclear physicist Vassili Nabokovski. McGreagor liked to tell the story about how he'd wooed both men from their former government positions to join NIISA, to pursue their shared dream of bringing commercial space travel to the world. The billionaire had convinced an array of fat cats to invest in his pipe dream. He hadn't told them that three of the private test flights had crashed and burned shortly after takeoff. That was something his new acquisitions were supposed to be looking into. Of course, those classified files from NASA that Turner had brought along with him were going to help. And Nabokovski had practically run the Soviet rocket program in the sixties and seventies.

Space experts, civilian commercial space travel, a city built on the moon, Hudson thought. What complete and total bullshit.

But the obnoxious Dr. McGreagor would soon see all his dreams crash and burn along with his failed rockets.

And I'll be a rich man, Hudson thought.

He smiled and thought of Kim Soo-Han's luscious body waiting for him in Mexico. It wouldn't be long now. Finding her had been a bit of good fortune. Not only would he be walking away from this deal a rich man, but he'd have the beautiful woman of his dreams to accompany him.

He smiled as his cell phone rang.

Glancing at the screen, he saw the call was from the big man himself.

Maintaining the charade, Hudson answered with a crisp, "How may I help you, sir?"

"Is the luggage loaded?" McGreagor asked.

The words were slightly slurred. Obviously, the festivities from the earlier party had continued into the pretake-off celebration.

"Yes, sir," Hudson replied. "And the crew's doing the preflight checklist now."

"I know that, you idiot. How much longer before take-off? My guests are anxious to get to Punta de las Sueños. I want to have everyone assembled on the beach to watch the sunrise."

"We should be in good shape, sir," Hudson said. "We'll get there in plenty of time."

"We had better," McGreagor threatened.

For all his bloviating about flight and space travel, the son of a bitch was totally oblivious to the safety requirements and procedures of a preflight inspection. Hudson resisted the temptation to use McGreagor's own platitude, "NIISA never skimps on safety," and instead replied, "I'll see how it's going and get back to you, sir."

"You do that," McGreagor said. "And you're sure you've gotten the appropriate security measures in place? I don't want any slipups on this trip. Understand?"

"Everything's in place, sir," Hudson said. More so than you know, he added mentally. He smiled again.

"And you have a sufficient supply of the local police? I want armed security on the beach perimeter."

"That's been taken care of, sir." And it had been. This was the only part of the plan that bothered Hudson a bit. He wouldn't be able to bring any of his guns into Mexico, and therefore allegedly had to rely on the local police for security concerns. While the police were more than happy to provide those services for the customary fee, this time Hudson knew that the officers had been recruited by Soo-Han's boss's cartel connection.

Though he trusted the woman, in the back of his mind he felt he needed some kind of an insurance policy. Trusting Soo-Han was one thing. Trusting her North Korean bosses was another. What was to stop them from stiffing him once the two scientists and the computer files for the new prototype reentry software were safely in their hot little Commie hands? Plus, North Korea wasn't exactly rolling in dough, with no exports to speak of except the bellicose ramblings of their leader and the threat to launch one of his nukes. What was to stop them from icing Hudson once their deal had been completed?

He needed an insurance policy, all right. Now all he had to do was figure out how to get one.

"Hudson, are you there?" McGreagor's tone had doubled in harshness.

"Yes, sir."

"Then, pay attention, dammit." McGreagor's words were getting more slurred. Hudson pictured him with a drink in his hand, scotch probably, and his toupee sagging as much as his facial muscles.

"I'm taking Irina with me," McGreagor said. "Make sure the crew has my private cabin ready."

Hudson knew that besides being McGreagor's traveling piece of ass, Irina was also his private nurse. The big man probably wanted her to get a bunch of Botox and other meds ready for the flight so he'd look ten years younger when they landed. But McGreagor was obviously so drunk now he'd forgotten that he'd given those instructions earlier.

"Already done, sir," Hudson said.

"What? Oh, okay." The boss paused, lowered his voice. "Listen, before we leave, make sure that everything's secure in research and development. Make sure everything's encrypted and in the vault, understand?"

"Absolutely, sir," Hudson said.

Encrypted, Hudson thought. I may have just found that insurance policy I was thinking about. "I'll see to it right away."

4

La Palacio de Oro Hotel
Culiacán, Sinaloa, Mexico

Bolan, Grimaldi and Martinez sat at a table in the hotel's café, a bowl of hard-boiled eggs at each place. The two Americans sipped their coffee while Martinez talked to his commanding officer on his cell phone. It had been a long night. Waiting for a contingent of high-ranking military and police officials from Mexico City to arrive had taken several hours, as had the interrogation of both Ruiz and Vargas. Neither man had given up much, saying only that if they talked, the cartel would kill them and their families. It had been enough for Bolan to expose the man who had betrayed them. It was now up to the Mexicans to clean their own house, but Bolan was curious about what the Cuban had told Stevenson and Chong. Both FBI agents had declined Martinez's offer of breakfast, saying that they had to go to the embassy to check in with their supervisor.

Martinez terminated his call and frowned. He set the cell phone on the table and shook his head. "Ruiz and his lackey still refuse to say much. What kind of world do we live in, my friends? Five of my men are dead and two traitors live."

"At least you discovered them," Grimaldi said. "I know it's not much consolation, but the leak's plugged."

"For the moment," Martinez said. He sighed and picked up his cup. "But I am certain they will break Ruiz once he goes to the capital."

"To the big house," Grimaldi said. "I'll bet he'll catch more than his lunch in there."

"Plus," Bolan said, "the agents of the cartels inside the prison will no doubt be expecting him. There's probably a contract out on him already."

Martinez nodded. "They will slit his throat in a matter of hours, once he is placed inside. The corruption is like a snake in the field, feasting on the mice." He drank the rest of his coffee and then stood, holding out his hand. "And now I must arrange transportation for the traitors to the capital."

Bolan and Grimaldi stood, as well. The men shook hands.

"You are a true warrior, my friend," Martinez said to Bolan. "It has been my honor to serve and fight beside you."

"The honor was mine," he replied, handing the sergeant a card. "You can always reach me through this number."

"I will keep you advised," Martinez said, pocketing it. He turned and left, and they watched him go.

Grimaldi emitted a low whistle. "Man, that big guy's pissed. I sure wouldn't want to be in old Ruiz's shoes."

"He lost a lot of good men due to Ruiz's treachery," Bolan said, as his cell phone rang.

He glanced at the screen and said to Grimaldi, "Looks like it's your FBI friends." Bolan pressed the button to accept the call.

"Cooper, this is Special Agent Chong. Where are you guys?"

"Still at breakfast in the hotel."

Chong said he and Stevenson were on their way and hung up.

"Looks like they want to talk," Bolan said. "They're coming here." He took out his sat phone. "I'm going to check in with Hal."

After a gruff hello, Brognola added, "You're up early."

"We haven't been to bed yet," Bolan said.

Brognola grunted as Bolan gave him a rundown of the previous night's events.

"So that's where we stand," the Executioner said. "I think we've plugged one leak down here as far as assisting the marines, but Chong and Stevenson still haven't told us what intel they got from the Cuban before he was killed."

"You say he was taken out with a karate blow?" Brognola asked.

"It was some kind of martial arts move," Bolan answered. "Jack says the waiter who delivered the room service was Asian, but he didn't get a real good look at him."

Grimaldi lifted his thumb in agreement and started to crack open another hard-boiled egg.

"Well, here's a little tidbit that might give you a clue or two," Brognola said. "There was an incident in the Panama Canal Zone last night."

That piqued Bolan's interest.

"Remember back a few months ago, when the Panamanians discovered a North Korean ship trying to smuggle some old Soviet-era ICBMs through the canal?"

"Right," Bolan said. "The missiles came from Cuba. Leftovers from the Cuban Missile Crisis."

"You got it," Brognola said. "The Koreans hid the missiles under a couple hundred sacks of sugar."

"And the Panamanians confiscated them under the authority of UN sanctions against North Korea," Bolan said.

"That's it in a nutshell. The sanctions forbid weapons to be sold to the bad guys up north of the thirty-eighth parallel." Brognola paused and cleared his throat. "Of course, the North Koreans immediately called the seizure an illegal action, and their leader started rattling his saber, which would be laughable if he didn't have the actual nukes to make it a little scary."

"More than a little scary if you're sitting in Seoul," Bolan said.

"Yeah, right," Brognola agreed. "As far as a credible threat to the US, he's lacking a long-range delivery system. But if they perfect the orbital reentry technology, he goes from regional boogeyman to hemispherical threat. All they're lacking is that software and the whole US is wide-open."

"And the reentry technology on the old Soviet missiles is going to give it to him?" Bolan asked. "It's more than fifty years old."

"You seen any photos of Havana lately?" Brognola asked. "Lots of '57 Chevys down there looking like new."

"Machines do seem to hold up well in that climate," Bolan said. "Maybe someone is maintaining the missiles. What were you going to tell me about last night?"

"Oh, yeah. Sorry. A few weeks back the ship's crew was released to North Korea. Who knows what happened to them? The Panamanians have been storing the missiles in a warehouse near the Canal Zone, awaiting further instructions. You know the glacial speed with which the UN moves, especially with the North Korean delegation raising a stink about things."

"Are you going to tell me that they did more than protest?" Bolan asked.

"A group of highly trained Asians hit the warehouse last

night," Brognola said. "Everybody's surmising it was them, but nobody can prove it. They incapacitated the Panamanian guards and moved the missiles out by truck."

"They left the guards alive?"

"Yeah," Brognola said. "That's the only thing that doesn't fit. Usually, the North Koreans don't leave any witnesses, so maybe they did it to throw off suspicion. But in any case, it's a no-brainer who they were. The conjecture is that sooner or later they'll admit it was them and say they were just recovering property that was illegally seized from them. Could that Asian guy you saw during the raid have been Korean?"

"Possibly," Bolan said. "Any idea where the missiles are now?"

"There are four known North Korean ships in the area at the moment. One is docked in Havana, purportedly to get another load of old Soviet ballistic missiles, which our man in Havana claims are on hand," Brognola said. "We're keeping tabs on that one."

"And the others?"

Brognola sighed. "The other three already passed through the canal during the past week, and are allegedly en route back to North Korea. Any one of them could have made a stop last night along the Panamanian coast for some special cargo."

"Do we have a fix on them?"

"Uh-uh. Apparently, they've turned off their transponders, which would help us locate them. Our navy's out looking, but…"

"It's a big ocean."

Three ships somewhere in the Pacific, one of which was carrying the stolen ballistic missiles. It was like a high-stakes version of the old shell game. Which shell was the prize under? Bolan's mind was racing, trying to put it all together, but it was like a jigsaw puzzle with all the pieces turned upside down. It was impossible to see how things fit together. How was the Mexican cartel involved with selling old missiles in Cuba to North Korea? Both countries were cash strapped. The Cubans weren't about to give anything away, even fifty-year-old missiles, and the North Koreans couldn't even buy their way into a penny-ante poker game. Who was footing the bill? And why send a special ops team to silence a Cuban informant, when it was obvious that the North Koreans had conducted the clandestine raid? Unless there was more to this whole game than was readily apparent.

"I don't like the way this is adding up," Bolan said. "I think we're missing a couple of real important pieces to the puzzle."

"You and I agree on that," Brognola said. "Want to stay down there and check it out?"

"Absolutely," Bolan said. He saw Chong and Stevenson getting out of a taxi in front of the café. "See what else you can find out about those missiles and get back to me. It looks like our FBI contacts are here now."

"Roger," Brognola said. "And watch yourselves. We both know that the North Koreans play hardball and don't hold back."

"Yeah," Bolan said. "But neither do I."

Culiacán International Airport
Culiacán, Sinaloa, Mexico

YI WATCHED AND waited as the rest of the Black Tigers proceeded through the customs line, getting their fake Chinese passports stamped. It reminded him of an assembly line at a factory, rote duties performed with lackluster effort. Soon they would all be through and free to embark on the next phase of the mission and the new complexities that had arisen. He had left two of his men in Panama to transport the Iranian, Farrokhzad, and the captive Mexican gangster by boat to the coastal resort. It would take them a few days, but the Iranian's yacht was comfortable. Plus a suitcase full of money would have raised too many questions at this airport, not to mention the additional problem of transporting the weapons.

Taking out his sat phone, Yi checked his watch and mentally calculated the time difference. It would be close to midnight, but he knew the general was a light sleeper. Besides, Yi was certain to be reprimanded if he failed to maintain his timely reporting. But first he removed his other cell phone and called the Dragon.

He answered on the first ring.

"Where are you?" Yi asked in Chinese.

"We are near the resort," the Dragon said. "We are awaiting your arrival so that we may all register together."

"Good."

"And you, sir?"

"We are clearing customs at the airport. Do you still have the equipment with you?" Yi asked, referring to the weapons that the cartel had provided to the Dragon to accomplish the neutralization of the Cuban.

"Yes."

"Good. The rest is being shipped to us," Yi said, thinking about the slow boat bearing the Iranian, the suitcase, the guns and the Mexican gangster. Although he regretted abandoning the weaponry in Panama, transporting weapons across international borders was too much of a risk. Yi thought about the disposal of the other excess baggage. He had killed the Panamanian and left his body in the verdant jungle. It had been the most satisfying personal interaction he'd had with the man. The Mexican gangster would be next, but only after he served his purpose and provided the right assistance here. Yi was certain the Mexican's cooperation could be obtained by pointing a pistol at him.

"We had a problem with our guides at the previous location," Yi said. "Thus, we must formulate a contingency plan for any possible complications moving forward."

"Understood, sir."

Yi told the Dragon that he would contact him shortly, and terminated the call. It was now time to call the general.

Song's phone rang several times, and Yi was on the verge of hanging up when the general's voice came on line. *"Yeoboseyo."*

He was speaking in Korean instead of Chinese. Even though the transmission had scramblers on it, the security protocol had been clear: only Chinese was to be spoken, which Yi now used.

"Ah yes, I have forgotten my manners," General Song said, switching to Mandarin Chinese. From the slurring sound of his words, it was obvious he had been drinking. Yi felt a tightening in his gut. He disliked drunks and forbade himself ever to indulge in any type of intoxicant. It was especially troubling to him that Song would be imbibing while such a crucial mission was ongoing. But still, discovering a weakness of his superior officer was not such a bad thing. Rather, it was information to be filed away for a future usage.

"How goes your trip?" Song asked.

"All goes well, sir. The packages have been sent to you. They should arrive in eight days' time."

"I should hope sooner than that." Song laughed. It wasn't a pleasant sound. "It is already tomorrow in Pyongyang."

Another slip, mentioning the capital. Had the general consumed so much liquor that his senses had deserted him?

"Do you not like my humor?" Song asked, his tone growing harsh.

Yi pondered his response. "I do appreciate it, sir."

"Then, why do you not laugh?"

Again Yi pondered an appropriate response. "I am afraid that I have little time for amusement."

Song grunted in approval. "Then, everything is proceeding as we planned? What of the other shipment? Is that on schedule?"

"It is, as far as I know," Yi said. He actually had several agents on the ship in Havana seeing to that acquisition, but it was nothing more than a diversion to draw the Americans' attention. The important shipment was already under way. Had Song lost sight of the specifics, the intricacies? "I will look into it."

"You will do more than that," Song said. "You will see to it personally."

The drunken fool's arrogant petulance could upset the entire plan, but Yi knew better than to argue.

"It shall be done, as you directed, sir," Yi said. "We are looking forward to completing our performance here, and returning home soon."

"I shall so advise our great leader," Song said.

The words hit Yi like a roundhouse kick. The drunken idiot had used terminology that could be directly associated with the North Korean leader.

"I am sorry," he said. "All is well, but I must go."

Without waiting for a reply, Yi terminated the call, not concerned or worried that he had just hung up on his superior officer. There was too much at stake to risk the drunken fool inadvertently divulging any more information, encrypted phone transmissions or not. For now, he had only the skill and expertise of the Black Tigers, and himself, to rely on in accomplishing their task, and failure was not an option. He knew that if something did go wrong, it would be him before the firing squad, not the incompetent General Song. Such was the burden of the dedicated soldier's mission.

In his mind's eye, Yi harkened back to the days of his

namesake, Yi Sun-Shin, at the helm of a powerful dragon ship, dependent only on the fierceness of his crew and the armament that adorned the vessel. Yi could almost see the waves parting, as if in fear of the mighty dragon's head hovering above the water. In such days, when iron men ruled, the throats of weak, drunken failures like Song would be slit, their bodies thrown overboard.

Soon, Yi thought, there would be a return to those times. A return to greatness for the homeland. A united homeland.

All that mattered now was the success of the mission, and there was much to do.

Punta de las Sueños
Culiacán, Sinaloa, Mexico

HUDSON WATCHED AS Soo-Han sat naked on the edge of the bed and spoke softly on her cell phone. They'd just finished having sex and he was feeling satiated and mellow. The nighttime arrival and drunken reveling on the beach to watch the sunrise had sent his adrenaline into overdrive. While McGreagor and the investors waded in the surf and pounded down drinks from the beachfront bar, it had been up to Hudson to arrange for the special patrols and assure that the entire area was secure. But he hadn't minded. It was like guarding the golden goose, and soon the gold would be his.

Kim put her hand over the phone and turned to Hudson. "There has been a slight change in plans," she said in English. "The colonel says there is a sudden, urgent matter that has come up elsewhere that must be attended to. Thus, delaying our business here."

Hudson knew the North Koreans were trying to grab more of the old Soviet ICBMs in Cuba. It made sense. They were likely thinking that once they had Nabokovski, he could probably just transplant the reentry device from the old missiles to the Korean's SCUDs. But they'd still want the updated designs from NIISA. Plus the Iranians were after the long-range missile technology, too. And they were the ones footing the bill.

"Not a problem," Hudson said. "The cruise isn't scheduled for four days."

She nodded and went back to speaking in her native tongue.

Hudson's mind raced, wondering what additional measures he needed to take to safeguard himself once Yi had the scientists and the designs for the reentry technology.

"Ask him when I'm going to get my money," Hudson said.

She shot him a sly glance and covered the receiver. "Do you not mean 'our money'?" She smiled and resumed talking in Korean. Whether or not she asked the question, he had no idea.

Kim ended her call and looked at him in an alluring fashion as she crawled toward him on all fours.

"So did you ask him about our money?" Hudson asked.

"Of course," she said, then added, "Soon. Very soon."

La Palacio de Oro Hotel
Culiacán, Sinaloa, Mexico

BOLAN AND GRIMALDI sat across the table from Special Agents Chong and Stevenson, but no one was talking. Bolan signaled the waitress for more coffee. When she'd left, the FBI agents exchanged glances.

"So who are you guys really?" Chong asked.

"We already went over that, didn't we?" Bolan said.

Chong stared at him for a few seconds, then laughed. "Come on, you guys aren't DOJ, are you?"

"We need to know who we're dealing with before we cooperate," Stevenson added.

Bolan looked at her. "Did you call that number I gave you?"

"Yeah," Chong said, his face cracking into a smile. "And they verified everything you told me. But you two don't operate like any DOJ agents I ever met. Like I said, who are you really? CIA?"

Bolan shook his head. "Let's just say we're all on the same side. The more we can share our information, the better off we'll all be."

The FBI agents again exchanged glances. Finally, Chong said, "Okay, but like I told you, this is still a Bureau case."

Bolan nodded.

"Okay," Chong said. "Right after you left the hotel room, Espinoza opened up. He said he was tired of playing around and wanted a deal in writing. We told him that he'd have to give us something first, and when he did, it blew our socks off. It involves some weapons being sold in violation of UN sanctions." The agent stopped. "I'm going to have to check with my supervisor before I can say more, but—"

"North Korea's buying old Soviet-era ballistic missiles from the Cubans," Grimaldi said. "We already know that."

Chong's mouth gaped.

"Look," Bolan said. "This will go a lot faster if we don't have to keep playing twenty questions."

"You guys are CIA," Chong said. "I knew it."

"How much do you know?" Stevenson asked.

Bolan glanced around. It was getting toward midmorning and the café was starting to fill up a bit, but the section where they were seated was still mostly empty. He leaned forward. "The Cubans sold the North Koreans five ICBMs from the 1960s. The shipment was intercepted in the Panama Canal when inspectors found the missiles concealed under bags of sugar. The Panamanians were keeping the confiscated cargo in a warehouse in the Canal Zone until last night."

"Until last night?" Chong repeated.

"A group of commandos hit the warehouse in a raid," Bolan said. "They took the missiles."

"Coincidentally," Grimaldi added, "there were a bunch of North Korean ships in this area that have since disembarked. One of them has to have those missiles on board."

"A bunch?" Chong asked. "How many?"

Grimaldi held up three fingers. "And it's a big ocean."

"Do we know which of the three has the missiles?" Stevenson asked.

"We're trying to determine that," Bolan replied.

"Damn," Chong said. "We weren't told anything about the raid or the ships."

"Welcome to the world of compartmentalized information," Grimaldi told him. "If the left hand knew what the right hand was doing…"

Chong looked deflated. "You guys obviously know a hell of a lot more than we do."

"We don't know everything," Bolan said. "Like who's footing the bill. Did Espinoza say anything about that?"

"Well," Chong said, "he did hint that he had more to say, but wouldn't elaborate. He wanted to get his deal set up and in writing first."

"There's a fourth North Korean ship docked in Havana," Bolan said. "The conjecture is that they're there to obtain more ICBMs."

Stevenson's brow furrowed. "So what does this mean?"

Bolan took out his sat phone. "We're going to make arrangements to go to Cuba to check things out."

Chong looked at him. "I thought I told you this is a Bureau case."

"So file your report," Bolan said. He paused and looked at the two special agents. One was Cuban-American, and the other Korean-American. They wouldn't be a bad addition to this little venture. "You want to accompany us?"

The two exchanged glances yet again. "We'll have to get authorization from our supervisor first," Chong said.

Grimaldi snorted and started to say something, but Bolan silenced him with a hard look.

"I can arrange it," the Executioner said, holding up his phone.

The special agents appeared indecisive for a moment, then Stevenson gave a quick nod.

Chong turned to Bolan and said, "Okay, we're in."

Bolan punched a number into his sat phone and Grimaldi snapped his fingers for the server.

"Ah, looks like we're all Havana bound," he said. "And I need a shot of tequila before I leave Mexico."

5

American Embassy
Havana, Cuba

The room was small and hot, especially with the windows closed. The bright afternoon sunlight spilled around the edges of the drawn opaque shades, and a constant stream of water flowed from what looked to be an antique showerhead, splattering into the equally antique bathtub a few feet away. Grimaldi sat on the bed, and Chong and Stevenson stood nearby as Bolan fieldstripped a 9 mm Tokarev pistol and checked the firing pin. It seemed in working order, but he wouldn't feel comfortable until he'd put some rounds through it, something he doubted he'd be able to do in this place. He looked at Grimaldi, who was holding his own Tokarev and frowning.

"What's the story?" Grimaldi asked, looking around the small room. "Where's our usual stuff?" The water was running in the shower to provide background noise.

The assistant to the ambassador, Ted Hertel, held his finger to his lips in a silencing gesture. "Keep in mind that down here, these relatively new, normalized relations are suspended by a thread." He was a tall, thin man with shaggy gray hair and wire-rimmed glasses. Bolan knew he had been with the State Department for many years and was actually a clandestine operative.

Hertel reached over and adjusted the water flow in the shower. "And also assume your conversations are being monitored at all times."

Grimaldi rolled his eyes and said, "This ain't our first trip to the rodeo."

Hertel grinned and pointed to Chong and Stevenson. "No, but I bet it's theirs."

The two FBI agents looked self-conscious and very much out of place. Neither said anything.

"Up until last year," Hertel continued, "this place was no more than another abandoned building in Havana. Now, after the normalization, it's an embassy." He gestured toward the running shower. "Hence our rather archaic approach to security matters."

"That still doesn't explain why you're sticking us with substandard equipment," Grimaldi said, pointing to the pistol. "I'm a SIG Sauer man from way back, and my partner prefers a Beretta 93-R."

Hertel lifted his arms toward the ceiling. "What part of what I just said about always assuming that Big Brother is listening didn't you understand?"

"Jack," Bolan said, looking at Grimaldi and holding up the Tokarev. "These will do fine. I'm assuming this is the standard, and not the exception down here?"

"The same kind as the Cuban police use," Hertel said. "They can be discarded in any street gutter and nothing will be traced back to us here."

Bolan nodded. Even though things had opened up diplomatically, they were still in one of the most repressive countries around. Any chance that weaponry could be traced back to the US would be fodder for the Cubans to scuttle the diplomatic efforts.

"We'll be careful," he said, and reassembled the weapon. He eased the slide forward and then inserted the magazine, leaving the chamber empty. It was best not to trust a weapon he had yet to fire. Bolan gestured toward Chong and Stevenson. "Got any toys for them?"

Hertel shook his head. "Sorry, what you see is what you get."

Bolan nodded again. It made sense. Giving out weapons to unfamiliar, untested personnel could produce disastrous results. This wasn't the time or the place for on-the-job training. Still, he felt the two FBI agents could handle themselves, at least for the short term. "What if we need more equipment?"

"Cuba Libre can help you with that," Hertel whispered.

"Who's our contact?" Bolan asked.

Hertel adjusted the water flow again, creating as much noise as he could, then leaned toward Bolan. "His name's Miguel. He's a nonregistered taxi driver who drives an old '57 Chevy. He'll contact you using the phrase, 'It's a perfect day for bananafish.' When he feels it's safe, that is. As I said, assume you're being followed and watched at all times."

Bolan nodded. "And our cover?"

"Journalists," Hertel said, reaching into the diplomatic pouch and withdrawing four sets of false passports and IDs. He grinned. "Which one of you is Matt Cooper?"

"That would be me," Bolan said.

"If we're journalists," Grimaldi asked, "what are we supposed to be doing down here?"

"What else? You're here covering Homer Glen's goodwill tour."

"Homer Glen." Grimaldi shook his head. "That guy

couldn't carry a football in a picnic basket. And now he's just another washed-up jock trying to be a movie star."

"Yeah," Hertel said, "but the Cubans love him."

Grimaldi stood, then inserted the magazine into his pistol. "I don't suppose you've got a range in this building where we could put a couple rounds through these things, do you?"

Hertel shook his head. "Like I said, this ain't the Ritz."

"Marvelous," Grimaldi said. "I guess I can always throw it, if it doesn't work."

Hertel laughed. "Sounds like a plan. Just keep in mind that the secret police are all over, watching and waiting, and there's usually an informer on every corner."

Bolan snapped the Tokarev into its holster and belted it into position.

Grimaldi sighed and did the same. "Anything else we have to watch out for?"

Hertel shrugged. "*Derrumbes*—building collapses."

"Building collapses?" Grimaldi repeated.

"Some of these structures are old," Bolan said, putting on his shirt and making sure the untucked tails covered the holstered weapon. "The tropical air has rotted a lot of the timbers in the buildings and there's no money to repair them."

Hertel raised his eyebrows. "I'm impressed. I take it you've been here before?"

"Secret police, informers and collapsing buildings," Grimaldi said. "Sounds like a piece of cake." He picked up one of the small suitcases with the video equipment and handed it to Chong. He picked up the second one and hefted it. "Hey, yours is lighter. How come I always end up doing the heavy lifting on these gigs?"

"Because you're so good at it," Bolan said, allowing himself a rare grin. "Come on, let's go catch a cab."

Punta de las Sueños
Culiacán, Sinaloa, Mexico

ENSCONCED IN THE booth at the far end of the lounge, Colonel Yi watched the figures on the dance floor several meters away in the softly lit bar. He felt uncomfortable in the blue polo shirt and tan slacks. The drink sat untouched on the table before him. His eyes drifted away from the dancers as he detected the movement of someone new entering the bar area.

Kim Soo-Han, accompanied by James Hudson, strolled into the lounge, and they were holding hands. While such overt physical contact would be frowned upon in the homeland, it was tolerable in this place, at this time. She was, after all, leading the man around like a goat about to be slaughtered.

Yi saw Kim surveying the room, but he made no gesture to summon her. Instead, he waited until she saw him. The two went to the bar, ordered drinks and began a casual walk toward the booths. When they got abreast of his table, Kim stopped and looked down at him.

"Why, Mr. Lee," she said. "I did not know you would be arriving here so soon."

"Please," Yi said, gesturing to the other side of the table. "Join me."

They sat, with Kim sliding into the area between them so the two men could look directly at each other across the table. Hudson appeared flaccid and pale. Yi sensed the man was both nervous and distrustful. Trying to seem reassuring, the colonel smiled.

"Let me buy you another drink," he said. "Or, perhaps, something to eat?"

Hudson shook his head. "I don't have much time. I have to arrange for some entertainment tonight."

"I see," Yi replied. "And what time will it be starting?"

"Around seven." He leaned closer. "Is Farrokhzad here yet?"

Yi shook his head. The Iranian was actually close by, but still on the boat. The timetable dictated that he be kept out of sight for the short-term.

Hudson looked around again. "When am I going to get my money?" he whispered.

His nervous actions were like a neon sign. Yi did not like that. He reached across and casually grabbed one of the man's fingers, twisting it slightly to cause Hudson to wince.

Yi smiled and leaned forward, as if he'd just been telling a very funny joke.

He increased the pressure on the finger. Hudson groaned, but did not cry out. Yi was satisfied that his power had been sufficiently demonstrated, so he released his grip. Hudson withdrew his hand and began massaging his finger.

"What did you do that for?"

"You must learn patience," Yi said. "And respect. Only then will we talk about your reward."

"Okay, just don't do that again. Please."

With the addition of that final word, a sign of weakness, Yi knew he had the man exactly where he wanted him. He smiled again.

"But of course," he said.

Plaza de la Revolución
Havana, Cuba

A GROUP OF tourists poured from their bus and began to walk down the street, talking and pointing, while their bilingual Cuban guide told them about the historic sites around the square.

"Over there," the guide said, pointing toward an old

domed building, "is what we call El Capitolio. Before the *triunfo*, the revolution, it once housed the government of the dictator, Fulgencio Batista, who was overthrown by our Fidel."

Bolan and company stood off to the side, observing and waiting. The tourists began to snap pictures, and Bolan signaled Grimaldi, Chong and Stevenson to turn away. The Executioner was certain that somewhere on the street the secret police were watching, and he didn't want anyone in his group photographed.

"Where is this Miguel guy?" Grimaldi whispered.

"Relax," Bolan said. "This was the pickup point Hertel gave us."

"I forgot how damn hot it is here in August," he replied.

"Have you guys been here before?" Chong asked.

Grimaldi smiled. "Kid, you'd be hard-pressed to find a place we haven't been to." He leaned close to Stevenson and said, "Hey, what do you say about the two of us meandering over to that bar over there and getting something cold to drink? The best Cuban beer is called—"

"I think that's our man," Bolan said, slapping Grimaldi's shoulder as a yellow-and-green vintage Chevy turned the corner and pulled slowly down the boulevard. Bolan glanced across the street and spotted two swarthy-looking men with dark mustaches, wearing loose-fitting, blue guayabera shirts and tan slacks, gazing their way.

"Don't look now," he added, "but I think we've got two guys checking us out."

"What do you want to do?" Grimaldi asked.

Bolan watched as the old Chevy crept closer. The man behind the wheel was also looking around warily.

"Come on," Bolan said, heading into the group of tourists. When the majority of the crowd was between them and the two secret policemen, Bolan motioned for his people to head down a narrow alley. They trotted between the buildings, suddenly engulfed in shadow. The alley led to another, with more buildings on the other side. One of them appeared to be in a semidemolished state, and Bolan remembered Hertel's warning about the collapses. He held up his fist for everyone to stop, and motioned for Stevenson to join him.

"Take off your running shoes," Bolan said. "And can you roll your blouse up and tie it so that your midriff is exposed?"

"I can," she said, unbuttoning the garment. "But what's going on?"

"You need to look more like a barefoot native," Bolan said. "You'll have to go back to the square and flag down Miguel in his Chevy. Lean in on the driver's door, like you're looking for a ride. Then have him pick us up on the next block."

"Got it," she said, slipping off her socks and running shoes. "I hate to lose these."

"Don't worry," Grimaldi said, bending to pick them up. "I'll keep them close to my heart." He knotted the laces together and hung the shoes around his neck.

"Thanks." She finished knotting the blouse under her breasts and spun. "How do I look?"

"Like a million bucks," Grimaldi said, grinning. Bolan held her at arm's length and assessed her. She was pretty, no doubt about that. In fact, a bit too much so. He squatted and grabbed a handful of dirt from the alley floor. Standing, he held out his open palm.

"Smear a bit of this on your face," he said. "You look too immaculate."

Stevenson dabbed her fingers in the dirt and made some streaks on her face. They looked like camo stripes. Bolan grinned and smoothed them out a bit, and then told her to put some of the remaining dirt on her blouse and jeans.

"Hey, let me know if you need any help with that," Grimaldi said, flashing a rakish smile.

"Your clearance isn't that high," Stevenson said lightly, patting the dirt on herself.

Bolan was impressed at her show of pluck in the face of danger.

"Okay, head out," he said, pointing Stevenson back the way they'd just come. "And remember, no English, only Spanish. You recall the password?"

"Yes, I do," she said, and began jogging down the alley.

As Stevenson disappeared from view, the men ran down the narrow alley, which opened onto another street. Soft rumba music emanated from a nearby café, and scores of makeshift stalls lined the doorways of the buildings, with vendors hawking everything from bootleg DVDs to kitchen appliances.

Bolan steered Grimaldi and Chong toward the nearest one. "Act like you're shopping," he said, glancing up and down the block. He saw no obvious secret police, but the place could be full of informers.

A couple kids approached them, begging for money and offering everything from cigarettes and cigars to co-operative young women. Bolan heard the sound of a car turning the corner and saw the yellow-and-green sedan heading down the block.

"Our ride's here," he said.

The Chevy stopped, and Bolan saw Stevenson in the front passenger seat, with a male about thirty-five years old behind the wheel, his teeth gleaming white beneath his bushy mustache.

"Hop in, amigos," the man said. "Or do you want me to tell you about bananafish?"

Bolan opened the right front door and motioned for Stevenson to slide over, while Grimaldi and Chong got in the back.

"Easy on those doors when you close them," the driver said. "She is very old."

"I never abuse a classic," Grimaldi said, closing the door with a delicate pull. Bolan closed his a bit harder, and motioned for the driver to get moving.

"I know, I know," the driver said. "I appreciate you not making it too obvious for the police back there. And especially sending such a *bonita señorita* to fetch me." He shot a grin at Stevenson as he shifted the lever on the column to second gear. "You can call me Miguel, by the way."

"Okay," Bolan said. "And right now I'd appreciate it if you took us out of here, away from prying eyes."

Miguel nodded, accelerated and shifted to third, constantly glancing into his rearview mirror. After a few minutes he slowed a bit and sighed. "I think we lost them."

"Good," Bolan replied. "What can you tell us about the North Korean ship that's docked in the bay?"

Miguel shrugged. "It's pretty big. Looks like a transport vessel of some sort. It's been there a few days. Want to go by and take a look?"

"Definitely," Bolan said. "Any scuttlebutt about why it's here?"

"The word on the street says that they are waiting to get another load of old Russian missiles." Miguel laughed. "Why they would want them, after all these years, no one can say."

"They already got one shipment a few weeks ago," Bolan said.

"Yes, but they say the workers didn't load enough sugar on top," Miguel said with a laugh. "They found them out when they went through the canal."

Bolan didn't say anything more. Cuba Libre had its own network, but apparently Miguel hadn't heard about the North Korean's latest action taking the missiles from Panama. The Executioner figured that information was on a need-to-know basis, and their primary focus was the ship docked in Havana Bay.

The Cuban downshifted to second and made a left turn.

"Miguel, you mentioned that word is the North Koreans are here to get more missiles?"

"Ah, yes. Until the fall of the Soviet Union, the Russians were supporting us, like a guilty parent sending money to his bastard child. When the Soviet Union collapsed, the money stopped and they pulled out completely, leaving a lot of stuff behind. Old cars, old missiles." He grinned.

"The missiles have been here a lot longer than that," Bolan said. "The Cuban Missile Crisis was in 1962."

Miguel nodded. Bolan knew that the Soviets had backed down fifty-plus years ago, and had abandoned their plans to build missile-launching sites in the Western Hemisphere. He also knew that although they'd left the missiles, they'd removed the nuclear triggers and fissionable material from them long ago, much to the Cuban leader's strenuous objections. Back then, even the Soviets knew the dangers of nuclear proliferation and leaving such a weapon in the hands of a ruthless dictator, although the Cuban strongman was purportedly heartbroken over losing the chance to become a nuclear power broker.

"So where are the missiles stored now?" Bolan asked.

Miguel made another quick turn and checked his mirrors again. "Just making sure our little friends are not behind us. What did you ask? Where the missiles are kept?"

"Right," Bolan said.

Miguel laughed. "On a little island our former leader discovered after the failed invasion by the US many years ago."

"How accessible is it?" Bolan asked.

"You can only get to it by boat or plane," Miguel said. "Helicopter patrols guard it day and night. And a private security force is kept on the island, one that can repel an invasion from the US Marines."

"That'll be the day," Grimaldi said. "Our men would eat those guys for breakfast."

"Perhaps so, perhaps not." Miguel shrugged, then flashed another wry grin. "But after fifty-four years, and now the new normalized relations, I no think we gonna find out who's right."

"Why are the missiles there?" Bolan asked. "And how are they stored?"

"Well, from what I have heard, it's a nostalgia thing, reminding an old man of former glory days."

"But he's selling them now?" Bolan asked. "To the North Koreans?"

"So they say." Miguel shrugged as he turned onto a broad avenue. "The ship is down this way. You can't miss it."

The view of the bay opened up before them, a long, vacant harbor with only one large transport ship docked in the center port.

Miguel slowed a bit as they passed the North Korean ship. It was a long transport vessel with a three-story bridge, and crew quarters on the aft section. Four derricks lined the starboard deck, and the triangular-shaped hull loomed over the water like the beak of a gigantic sea monster, waiting to pounce. The top half of the ship was painted jet-black, with big white Korean characters emblazoned just under the pointed beak. Halfway down, the black changed abruptly to a rusty, reddish brown, indicating that the vessel was floating high and had yet to be loaded with any cargo.

"Any idea how many are in the crew?" Bolan asked.

"At least thirty," Miguel said. "They have been patronizing the bars, and the girls, for the past few nights. Word is they are set to leave soon, much to the chagrin of the local bar owners. From what I hear, they have been very good customers."

That didn't sit right with Bolan. Not that sailors from any nation wouldn't show a tendency to overspend and overindulge, but North Koreans didn't have that kind of money. Once again, it came down to the question of who was paying the tab.

"What money are they using?"

"They have CUCs," Miguel said, citing the most valuable of the Cuban currency. "Again, I have heard that they have a lot of euros and US dollars to trade, too."

"Do the Koreans have anybody with them?" Bolan asked. "Any non-Asians?"

"Funny you should ask that," Miguel said. He pushed the gearshift into second and accelerated away from the ship. "I don't like to dawdle, as they say. Too many prying eyes around." He made a sharp left turn and started driving away from the waterfront.

"You were saying?" Bolan asked, minutes later.

"*Sí*, definitely not Asian. There is one man. He looks like he could be European, perhaps from *la España*. Dark hair, mustache. He stays on the ship most of the time, but has been seen getting into a car that picks up him along with a couple of the others."

"What kind of car?"

"Limo," Miguel said, patting his shoulder in a manner to indicate a braided epaulet. "A car of *los peces gordos*. The fat fish. The secret police."

"How many times have they seen him leave?"

"Two times. The first was the day they arrived. The second was earlier today, and that time he had a big suitcase with him."

"A suitcase?"

"*Sí*." Miguel rubbed his thumb and forefingers together. "The kind that can hold *mucho dinero*."

It was starting to make sense. The North Koreans had someone who was footing the bill. Bolan remembered the recovered suitcase from the Mexican raid. At least that part of the purchase had been intercepted. Perhaps that was why the ship was still moored here and not loading the missiles on board. Bolan felt the need to check in with Brognola and give him a sitrep, as well as figure their next move, whatever that might be. He also wondered if the North Koreans were doing the same.

6

Punta de las Sueños
Culiacán, Sinaloa, Mexico

Hudson's fingers still felt sore from that asshole, Yi, bending and twisting them. Damn, that Korean was strong. He had hands like vise grips. Hudson watched as McGreagor continued to make the rounds at the pool, laughing and joking with his guests. He was wearing swimming trunks and a baggy green shirt, his sweat already making half-moon circles under each arm. He looked around for a server and pointed to his now empty glass. The man approached him and bowed. "What are you drinking, sir?"

"Scotch on the rocks," McGreagor said. The server nodded and left.

The billionaire's gaze searched out and met Hudson's. The big man made a quick beckoning gesture, his impatience obvious.

Hudson strolled over, making sure to watch his step as he moved past the pool. One of the young ladies was on the diving board, teasing, about taking off her top.

When he approached, McGreagor leaned close. "Go

to my room and fetch me a clean shirt," he said, reaching into his pocket. "Here's my key."

It was the moment Hudson had been hoping for—a chance to break away from McGreagor and get to his own room. Although Hudson had already downloaded the schematics and plans for the new reentry technology, his little thumb-wrestling match with Colonel Yi had added a new level of anxiety to their transaction. Hudson was concerned with how easily the colonel had incapacitated him. The asshole was a walking assassin, and from what Kim had said, the younger, muscular guy that Yi had brought along was some sort of North Korean superman. All that left little doubt that once the Koreans had the scientists and the schematics, their pledge to make Hudson a very rich man would be worth about as much as a three-dollar bill.

No, he needed that insurance policy, something to give him the upper hand when dealing with these Asian gangsters. He accepted the key from McGreagor and said with a smile, "Yes, sir. I'll be right back."

FROM THE ROOF of the building, Yi peered through his binoculars and watched the Americans and the Mexican women frolicking in the pool. The rich American, McGreagor, had reserved that area for himself and his associates for the afternoon. Official notice had been given, and the resort had graciously apologized to the other guests for any inconvenience, saying that the pools on the other side of the building were available for their pleasure. Portable barriers and privacy screens had been placed around the enclosure, which had immediately sent Yi to the roof to observe the proceedings. The decadent display did little to impress him, and he noticed Hudson standing by in silent vigilance.

Had twisting Hudson's finger been a mistake? The man seemed more nervous now, and more anxious. He had been recruited and kept in line very nicely by Kim Soo-Han, so perhaps the show of force Yi had used was unwise. Still, the man's insolence and audacity had rubbed Yi the wrong way. It had seemed necessary to instill in him a bit of fear and respect, as it had with the Mexican and Panamanian gangsters.

Yi thought about the captive Mexican. The boat should be arriving soon, and he needed to keep the Mexican cartels at bay until the abduction of the scientists was complete and the missile reentry plans were in his possession. Then the Mexican's throat could be slashed, and he could be dumped overboard. If the cartel complained later, it would not matter. Yi's dealings with these dishonorable thieves would be over. Hudson, too, would be meeting a similar fate. The fate of all traitors.

Yi brought up the glasses and saw Hudson leaving the pool area after accepting something from his boss.

Yi wondered where he was going, and thought again that the finger twisting had indeed frightened the rabbit and perhaps made him more wary.

I must be certain that Hudson has no method with which to betray me, Yi thought.

Hotel del Blanco
Havana, Cuba

BOLAN DID A quick scan of the room with his cell phone to check for any listening devices, and found none. To be extra certain, Grimaldi looked toward Chong and held his finger to his lips. He went into the bathroom and turned on the shower, then to the television set, and turned that on, as well. The screen illuminated after a solid forty seconds, and the image of American former-football-player-turned-wannabe-movie-star Homer Glen filled the screen.

"I want to say," Glen said in his deep voice, "that I have nothing but the utmost respect for the Cuban president and his brother. What they've accomplished here in Cuba has been nothing short of amazing."

Grimaldi smirked and held up his middle finger. "That chump must've gotten tackled one time too many."

Chong laughed. "You guys are something else."

The door opened and they all whirled, only to see Stevenson storm in.

"The shower's not working in my room," she said, heading for the small bathroom. "Oh, good, you've got this one warming up for me."

"Now isn't such a good time," Grimaldi said.

"Oh, I suppose you want to jump in ahead of me and use up what little hot, or should I say warm, water there is in this fleabag hotel?"

"Better leave the door open," Grimaldi said with a grin. "Security."

She rolled her eyes and stepped past him.

"And let me know if you need your back scrubbed," he added as she slammed the door.

"Hey," Grimaldi said, reopening the door. "I told you to leave it open."

Bolan had his sat phone out and was about to contact Brognola. "Give her some space, Jack. She's had a rough morning."

The big Fed answered on the first ring. "I think this is the first time we've been in the same time zone in a long while."

"I'll try not to get used to it," Bolan said. He gave Brognola an update on the situation and the North Korean ship in the harbor. "We still haven't figured out who's footing the bill, though."

"That would be nice to know," the big Fed said. "But I'm sure we can narrow it down to a few of the usual suspects. You say the Cubans have more missiles down there?"

"That's what they say. Supposed to be at a secret island hideaway."

"Hmm, do you think you could put a designated hitter on that vessel?"

"Maybe," Bolan said, knowing that Brognola was referring to a transponder. "Know where I can find one?"

Brognola laughed. "As a matter of fact, I do. Go see Ted."

"He's been pretty stingy with equipment. Our two newbies are running around naked."

Bolan was certain that the sat phone transmission was encrypted and totally secure, but he wasn't so sure about their hotel room. Thus, he didn't press Brognola for too much information, and sensed that the big Fed, well schooled in the art of espionage, was doing the same.

"Yeah, I know." Brognola sighed. "He's not a bad guy, just caught between the rock and the hard place. State's insistent on treating Cuba with kid gloves. I'll make a call and see if I can loosen things up for you."

"Any word on the three missing ships?"

"We're still looking. The USS *Reagan* is in the area, ready with a contingent of SEALs, who've been training for a boarding party if and when they get the chance."

"That's one party I wouldn't mind being invited to," Bolan said.

Brognola laughed. "I'll see what I can do. Like I said, it's a big ocean, but the trip's a long one. The estimate is about eight days, unless they've got some kind of supership."

"If they left that night, we're coming up on the forty-eight-hour mark."

"Yeah, but we're pulling out all the stops. We'll find them. You just try to get me a designated hitter on that baby down your way. You got any ideas about how feasible that might be?"

Just then Stevenson threw back the shower curtain, swore loudly when she saw the open door and closed the curtain again. Moments later she walked out of the bathroom wearing a towel and nothing more, while running a comb through her hair.

Grimaldi emitted a loud wolf whistle.

She paused to give him the finger.

"What the hell's going on down there?" Brognola asked.

"Jack's just being Jack," Bolan said, snapping his fingers for Grimaldi to turn the water back on.

The pilot stepped around Stevenson, entered the bathroom and twisted the faucets, dodging the wet clothes she'd left hanging over the shower rod.

Brognola chuckled again. "Well, it's good to know that no matter where you guys are, some things never change."

Like the War Everlasting, Bolan thought.

"So as I was saying," Brognola continued, "do you have any ideas about the designated hitter?"

Bolan looked at Stevenson and then at Chong, who was smiling ear to ear.

"Yeah," Bolan said. "I have an idea. I'll get back to you."

Punta de las Sueños
Culiacán, Sinaloa, Mexico

HUDSON GLANCED AT his watch and, despite the air-conditioning, felt a trickle of sweat work its way down the center of his back. He wiped his forehead and continued with this last task. McGreagor's clean shirt lay on the table a few feet away, and Hudson hoped this quick detour into his own room would not attract too much suspicion. It was necessary. He'd downloaded the files for the reentry plans from the NIISA main computer three days ago, converted each page into a PDF, encrypted them and then transferred them to the flash drive. His original intention was to give the small, easily concealed object to Yi in exchange for the payment. But after the finger-twisting session he realized how easy it would be for the colonel to merely take the drive and not deliver on the payment.

Now it had become a matter of trust, and Hudson trusted the burly Korean about as far as he could throw him. So he was quickly assigning a password to each PDF page, long passwords that he had no hope of remembering, even if Yi decided to beat the hell out of him. Instead, he copied and pasted each one into a separate file, along with the encryption code, which he stored on his laptop. That would afford him a bit of wiggle room, as long as Yi didn't get hold of the laptop. Hudson could email the passwords once he'd received his money and effected a safe getaway. Yi would need the passwords before he could open the reentry files.

It had taken Hudson a bit longer than he'd anticipated. He estimated he'd been gone close to fifteen minutes, and McGreagor didn't like to be kept waiting. Not that Hudson gave a shit about the rich man's whims, but he didn't want to do anything overly suspicious that might upset the applecart at this late stage.

He felt the sweat seeping through the armpits and front of his shirt as he transferred the last of the passwords to the file, secured that with another password and shut down the machine.

Yi would never be able to open the files unless Hudson gave him the information, and that would be done only when the colonel and his men were far, far away. The insurance policy was now in effect.

Hudson carefully replaced his laptop in the room safe and stood.

Nineteen minutes and counting. McGreagor was going to be livid, and Hudson knew that the old prick would no doubt chew him out in front of everyone poolside. His boss loved to throw his weight around.

But soon that won't matter, Hudson thought. Soo-Han and I will be long gone.

He stripped off his now sodden shirt and grabbed a fresh one from the dresser. He used one of the towels from the bathroom to wipe the sweat from under his arms, and slipped on the new shirt.

Soon, he thought, and opened the door, to find Kim, Colonel Yi and that scary-looking dude they called the Black Dragon standing there.

"We have much to talk about," Yi said, his face devoid of emotion.

Outside the Hotel del Blanco
Havana, Cuba

BOLAN WATCHED AS Ted Hertel meandered around the public square in front of the hotel, ostensibly perusing the haphazard stacks of bootlegged merchandise the doorway vendors were offering. Hertel looked relaxed and casual in a straw hat and sunglasses, and he carried a brown paper shopping bag in his left hand. Bolan punched a number into his burner cell phone and watched as the slender Agency man nonchalantly reached into his pocket and took out his own.

"I trust your ride with Miguel went well?" Hertel said without preamble.

"It did," Bolan replied. "And am I to assume from your outfit that you're concerned about prying eyes?"

"That's always a safe bet, which was why this next contact needs a bit of finesse."

"She's on her way," Bolan said, watching as Stevenson slowly walked toward the Agency man.

"Good. I don't mind getting ripped off by a real babe." Hertel laughed. "Catch you later."

Bolan placed the cell phone back into his pocket and picked up an old coffeepot from the blanket on the ground in front of the nearest vendor, who immediately began expounding on the virtues of the item. The Executioner pretended to listen as he kept surreptitiously watching Hertel and Stevenson. The Agency man set his bag on the street, picked up a bootlegged DVD from a stack and began conversing with the vendor in Spanish. Stevenson, who was close by, stopped, picked up the bag and began to walk away.

No one took much notice of things. Stevenson strolled toward the hotel. Hertel continued his bartering with the Cuban vendor, and then they both laughed. He set the DVD back on the stack, made a show of looking for the shopping bag and swore. After a quick shrug, he slowly sauntered down the street. Bolan waited until Stevenson disappeared inside the hotel. No one followed.

"Hey, American," the Cuban vendor said to Bolan, pointing to the coffeepot. "You gonna buy it or no?"

"No," Bolan said, and turned back toward the hotel. He stopped again just inside the entry and turned, partially concealed by the ornate door screens.

No one was watching; no one followed him.

The Executioner went inside and walked over to the elevators. All four doors were closed, and the arrow indicator showed all were in use. Bolan pressed the button and waited, casually turning to glance at the entrance.

One of the two swarthy Cuban secret policemen Bolan had seen earlier on the street, before they'd lost them and gotten into Miguel's cab, came in, removed his sunglasses and surveyed the lobby. Bolan stepped behind a large potted plant, apparently just in time. The man strode over to the hotel desk, flashed some credentials and began to question the clerk. They were too far away for Bolan to hear anything, but from the looks of it, the policeman was grilling the hotel employee about something.

The elevator doors opened, but Bolan remained where he was. The conversation between the two Cubans continued for a minute or so longer. Finally, the policeman gave instructions to the clerk, emphatically pointing with his index finger, before replacing his sunglasses on his face, turning and walking out the front doors.

If the hotel staff was in collusion with the secret police, Bolan thought, he would have to make an adjustment to their plans for later that night.

Punta de las Sueños
Culiacán, Sinaloa, Mexico

HUDSON WAS CONSCIOUS of Soo-Han, Yi and the Dragon walking close behind him as he made his way to the pool. Yi's sudden appearance had startled Hudson, making him start to sweat all over again. The colonel's dark stare had totally unnerved him, and that Dragon character scared the hell out of him.

"What are you doing?" Yi had asked. "Why did you leave the pool area?"

Hudson was flustered, but quickly explained his mission to fetch a clean shirt, hoping that Yi would surmise that this did not affect their arrangement.

"It's part of my job," he said. "We can't afford to make McGreagor suspicious, can we?"

Yi's expression didn't change, nor did the Dragon's. Both of them merely stood there blocking Hudson's way back to the pool.

Kim said something in rapid-fire Korean. Yi's expression still didn't change, his dark eyes seeming to cut into Hudson's flesh.

"Perhaps," Yi finally said, "it is time you introduce us to Mr. McGreagor."

That shocked Hudson. The last thing he wanted to do was introduce the North Koreans to the man whose secret technology and top scientists they were going to steal.

"I don't think that's such a good idea," he said. "What if he gets suspicious?"

"He will not," Yi replied. "Introduce us as rich Chinese, here on a business venture. I am certain Mr. McGreagor would always welcome another possible investor."

Hudson realized he had no choice. McGreagor would already be steamed about his tardiness running the errand. But maybe this could work. The original plan had been for the scientists to be taken at gunpoint from their rooms, but if he could get McGreagor to welcome Yi and company into the investors' fold, perhaps even invite them on the upcoming cruise, they would have more options for a smooth abduction of Turner and Nabokovski.

"All right," Hudson said. "Follow me."

As they walked past the guarded entrance to the pool, Hudson saw that McGreagor was indeed livid at the long delay in getting a fresh shirt. His head shot up, a look of barely subdued rage on his face as he jumped to his feet and strode over to Hudson and the Koreans. Their presence, however, apparently kept his boss from making a scene.

"Took you long enough," McGreagor said. "Where the hell have you been? And who are they?"

Hudson smiled as benignly as he could. "Sorry, sir. I had to change my shirt, too." He pinched some of the material between his thumb and forefinger.

McGreagor frowned and glanced at Yi and the Dragon, but let his eyes linger on Kim's luscious body. She was wearing a transparent white silk kimono over a leopard-print bikini. "Who are they? This is a closed party."

"I ran into Mr. Lee and his friends in the lobby," Hudson said. "He's from China. We met each other when I was down here earlier this week, and he expressed a desire to meet you." Hudson held his hand in front of his chest and rubbed his fingers together, signifying money.

McGreagor canted his head. "Oh?"

I've got him intrigued, Hudson thought. He quickly added, "Mr. Lee is here on business, but was very interested in hearing more about NIISA."

McGreagor smiled as he pulled off his sweaty shirt, wadded it up and handed it to Hudson. After slipping into the new one, he extended his hand toward Yi.

"It's a pleasure to meet you, sir. What part of China are you from?"

Yi accepted the hand, shook it and made a slight bow. "My company is based in Shanghai," he said. "This is my personal assistant, Miss Kim, and my head of security, Mr. Park."

McGreagor shot a quick nod at Kim as he extended his hand toward the Dragon, who shook it and bowed.

Hudson's boss recoiled in pain, pulling his hand away and shaking it. "Wow, he's got quite a grip, doesn't he?" McGreagor said with a smile.

Yi said something to the Dragon in a language that Hudson assumed was either Chinese or Korean. Kim laughed and the Dragon bowed again.

"Please accept our humble apologies," Yi said. "Mr. Park sometimes forgets his strength when dealing with others. He is very formidable."

"That I believe," McGreagor said.

"Perhaps a little demonstration of Mr. Park's skill might prove amusing for your guests," Yi suggested, extending his palm toward the group of partygoers.

McGreagor's face wrinkled into an expectant expression. "Sure. Why not? What's he going to do?"

Yi turned to the Dragon and issued some orders.

The Dragon nodded and moved over to the bar area, with Kim trailing behind him, and pointed to a bottle of bourbon on the platform next to the bartender.

"Would you give us that unopened bottle, please?" she asked.

The bartender looked perplexed as he glanced at McGreagor.

"Give it to them," the billionaire ordered.

The man shrugged and handed the bottle to Kim, who in turn gave it to the Dragon. He hefted the bottle in his hands, as if estimating the weight and density, then glanced around. The Dragon said something inaudible to Kim, handed the bottle back to her, and they walked to some tables adjacent to the pool area.

Yi stepped next to McGreagor. "What Mr. Park will do," he said, "is demonstrate the efficiency of his martial arts capability."

Kim held the bottle up for everyone to see, while the Dragon carried one of the metal tables as far from the pool as he could, stopping at the metal fence. The area was all concrete. Kim placed the bottle in the center of the table and stepped back, like a magician's assistant in a sideshow. The Dragon stepped behind the table, positioning himself so that he faced everyone, and glanced at Yi.

"Mr. Park will now show you a new way to open one of your bottles," the colonel said. He gave a quick nod.

Hudson watched as the Dragon assumed a squatting stance and cocked his right arm back. A blurring movement followed a second later and the edge of the Dragon's hand struck the neck of the bottle, skimming it off as if it had been cut by a laser. The fragment jumped in the air, and he twisted and caught it with his left hand before it could fall to the tabletop. The remainder of the bottle stood undisturbed.

A collective gasp went through the crowd, followed by a smattering of applause.

Yi gave a curt nod to the Dragon, who immediately picked up the unbroken bottle and the severed top and brought them to McGreagor. Kim trailed behind.

The rich man's face had an ear-to-ear grin. "Amazing," he said, reaching for the two items. "Simply amazing."

"Be careful, Mr. McGreagor," Kim said. "The broken glass can be dangerous. We do not wish you to injure yourself."

"Neither do I," McGreagor said with a laugh. He glanced around, obviously enjoying the stunned reaction of his guests. Then he turned to Yi. "Mr. Lee, I think this is the beginning of a great partnership."

Yi smiled and nodded. "So do I." As he turned, his eyes shot toward Hudson in a calculated glance.

Hudson watched McGreagor hold the broken bottle top in his hand, a look of awe and admiration on his face. "Maybe I should fire you, Hudson, and hire this guy."

You arrogant, rich son of a bitch, Hudson thought. If you only knew what's coming.

7

Hotel del Blanco
Havana, Cuba

As dusk was descending, Bolan opened the window of
their hotel room and tossed out the thin nylon line, watching it uncoil as it fell in the semidarkness. He was dressed
in a combat blacksuit and had on lightweight tactical boots.

Grimaldi secured the end of the rope around the bed
frame and tested the knot. "Looks good," he said, standing.

Bolan slipped on his gloves and fitted the D ring
through the Swiss seat he'd fashioned from a length of
nylon. He checked the Tokarev pistol he had secured in a
nylon holster on his belt. He had two extra magazines in
a holder on the opposite side.

"Just in case," the Executioner said, "why don't you sit
on the bed to give it more weight?"

Grimaldi grinned and plopped down on the mattress,
patting the surface and looking at Stevenson. "Want to
join me?"

Chong sat next to him with a wide smile and said,
"Sure."

Stevenson smiled, too, but then the space between her eyebrows wrinkled. "Are you sure about doing this?"

Bolan didn't answer. He simply moved to the window and slid the rope through the D ring.

"Don't worry," Grimaldi said. "He does this kind of thing all the time. He's actually got a big red *S* on his chest."

Bolan looked at Stevenson. "I'll call when I get back. Be ready."

She bit her lower lip and nodded.

The Executioner climbed out the window, braced himself on the outside edge and leaned backward until his head was lower than his feet. He shoved off and felt himself sailing downward, controlling his descent, bouncing lightly off the wall every twenty feet or so, carefully avoiding the other windows. Ironically, he was reminded that this was the same way the North Korean assassin had escaped after killing the Cuban in Mexico.

Approximately thirty seconds later Bolan was on the ground. He tugged on the rope twice and felt it being pulled upward. Confident that Grimaldi would take care of that task, Bolan untied the Swiss seat, rolled it up and stuck it and the D ring into his pocket. He'd landed in an alleyway behind the hotel. It was not quite dark enough to conceal his movements, but he'd assumed that the Cuban police would be busy watching the lobby and maybe the rear exit, but would not be standing in the hot night air of the alley. A quick look up and down confirmed that.

Bolan strode to the opening of the alley and stopped. He glanced both ways and, seeing no sign of the police, turned right and walked at a leisurely but steady pace to the next block. The '57 Chevy was parked at the curb, with Miguel behind the wheel, smoking a cigarette. He winked and nodded as Bolan got in.

"Ah, amigo, you right on time," the Cuban said as he

started the car and shifted into first. Before pulling away, he scanned the area. "I know you're good, but I gotta check to make sure the police didn't follow you."

They rode in silence for a time, with Miguel checking the rearview mirror after each turn. Finally, they arrived at the harbor. The big North Korean ship sat in isolation at the pier.

"It's still here, amigo," Miguel said.

"Check with your men and see if the crew's started disembarking for liberty yet," Bolan said.

Miguel took out his cell phone and punched in some numbers. After a few moments of low conversation, he turned back toward Bolan. "They are just starting to leave now. There is a guard at the gangplank checking who is going. He looks like a Korean."

"How diligent is he?" Bolan asked.

Miguel squinted. "Diligent? Oh, you mean how *serio*?" He spoke into the phone again, then smiled. "He no look too close when they leave. Maybe he gonna be more careful when they go back. And they already took about ten pretty *señoritas* onto the ship. Apparently, the captain and ship officers want to be amused."

Bolan considered that. If there was a party atmosphere on the ship, Chong had a good chance to slip on board, plant the transponder and get off without being noticed. But perhaps the guard would be more vigilant monitoring people trying to get back on the ship. Their plan would still require the diversion.

"Which building is it?" Bolan asked, glancing at the unlit structures lining the side of the street opposite the harbor.

"That one," Miguel said. "My amigos already spread the word to stay away from there tonight."

"And you've got the explosives?"

Miguel laughed. "*Sí*, Cuba Libre's got plenty of stuff.

We sit and wait and clean our guns until the next Bay of Pigs invasion. It will be a pleasure to finally use them."

He told Miguel to drive past the ship. As they rolled down the avenue, Bolan watched as groups of North Koreans began disembarking from the freighter. Most walked in groups, but some were by themselves. They wore motley civilian clothes, and most had their hair slicked back on top and short on the sides. As he and Miguel drove past, Bolan took out his burner cell phone and called Grimaldi, who answered, "What's the good word?"

"It looks like a go," Bolan said. "But get a pair of scissors and cut Chong's hair on the sides. High and tight. Then have him slick back what's left on top."

Grimaldi laughed. "You know, I had an uncle who used to be a barber."

"Let's hope the talent runs in the family. Also, tell Stevenson to get ready. I'll be back in approximately ten minutes."

"Roger that," Grimaldi said.

Bolan clicked off and told Miguel to take him back to the hotel. It was time to get things rolling before the North Korean's Cinderella Liberty ended.

Punta de las Sueños
Culiacán, Sinaloa, Mexico

As COLONEL YI relaxed in his comfortable room, he decided to allow himself the luxury of smoking an American cigarette. Such an act was forbidden in the homeland, but he considered it one of the small rewards for doing his country's bidding in a foreign land. He picked up the pack of Marlboros that he'd taken from a poolside table and shook one out. After tapping it a few times, he placed it between his lips and lit it. The smoke tasted mild compared to harsh tobacco he was used to. He drew on the cigarette again, and had to admit that the Americans did know something about refining tobacco.

Perhaps, Yi thought, once the mission was finished, he would imbibe some of the liquor that the American, McGreagor, had tried to force upon him. He had politely refused, pretending to have a stomach problem. The man had fallen for the ruse.

The Dragon stood by at silent attention, looking like a statue. He neither smoked nor drank alcohol, dedicated as he was to his physical conditioning. Yi admired the man's discipline, as well as his consummate martial arts skills.

Yi inhaled more smoke and took out his sat phone, deciding to call the ship's captain in Cuba. He wanted to verify that Lieutenant Yoon, whom he had dispatched over twenty hours ago to supervise the missile transaction in Cuba, had arrived. Yi punched in the numbers and listened. The phone rang several times before someone answered. The voice sounded slurred. Had the captain taken his duties so lightly that he would consume alcohol before the mission had been completed?

Yi heard what sounded like a woman's laughter, followed by a hushing sound. What was going on aboard that vessel?

"This is Colonel Yi. What is your status?"

"Everything is good," the captain said. "Very good. We await the arrival of your men. In the meantime—"

"What?" Yi said. "My men have not yet arrived?" He felt a burning fury rise within him at the drunken idiot's incompetence, not to mention the inefficiency of his own men, led by Lieutenant Yoon. Or had something untoward happened, preventing Yoon from making it to the ship?

Regardless, Yi thought, he will pay for his tardiness. "You sound inebriated," Yi said. "Have you been imbibing? And are there women aboard?" He heard the other man belch and that infuriated him even more. "You will answer me now."

"I—I may have…" the captain sputtered. "But I am totally within my capabilities."

Yi said nothing, letting his silence speak volumes. Finally, he snapped, "I am going to contact Lieutenant Yoon and find his estimated time of arrival. You will be ready to depart for the island as soon as he arrives."

"But the men are on liberty," the captain said.

"Liberty?"

"Yes, it is not often they get to experience the pleasures of a foreign port that is so friendly. And the Ira—"

"Watch what you say, you drunken fool!" If the Americans were listening, if they happened to pick up this conversation, the inadvertent comment that the Iranians were involved could jeopardize the entire operation.

"Our benefactor has been most generous," the captain continued. "And the women here are very beautiful."

"I care nothing for your carnal desires," Yi said. "And our leader will not take kindly to you putting your personal pleasures above your duty." He paused again, letting his words sink in. "How soon can you assemble your crew and be ready to depart for the island?"

The captain sputtered. "Many will have been drinking. I don't—"

"They are your men," Yi shouted. "Maintain proper discipline of your crew, or upon your return you will be held accountable for your lax attitude toward command and responsibility."

Yi heard the other man gasp. "Yes, sir. Of course. It shall be done, just as you order."

Again, Yi let silence speak for him. After a long ten seconds, he said, "I will phone you back."

He terminated the call and punched in the numbers for

Lieutenant Yoon's sat phone. The man answered immediately. "Yes, sir."

"Where are you? And why have you not made it to the ship yet?"

"We are almost there, sir," Yoon said, his voice full of deference. "We were delayed at the airport."

"I am not interested in excuses," Yi replied. "Only results. Proceed to the ship. That drunken fool of a captain has been remiss in his duties. Assess everything and report back to me. You will leave for the island forthwith. Do you understand?"

"Yes, sir," Yoon replied.

"Remember, I do not tolerate fools or failure. Call me back once you are under way."

Outside the Hotel del Blanco
Havana, Cuba

BOLAN WATCHED AND waited in the shadows as Grimaldi, Stevenson and Chong exited the hotel. Chong's new haircut looked terrible, but hopefully he could pass for a very drunk North Korean sailor. The two men laughed loudly, keeping Stevenson nearly concealed between them. They turned right, ambling down the block at a slow pace.

One of the mustachioed national policemen slipped out the front entrance and gave a quick wave. Two more police officers, who'd been stationed across the street, began to follow the trio.

The first man moved over to the pillars in front of the hotel and took out his cell phone. While he was dialing, Bolan embarked on an intercept course for the two trailing officers. At the corner, he moved across the street and glanced quickly down the block. He was certain he was out of view of the man stationed by the front doors.

The happy trio continued their stroll, laughing and talking. The two Cuban policemen followed at a reasonable distance, so as not to be too conspicuous. Bolan had his cell phone set to call Grimaldi's number. He pressed the button, knowing that his partner would feel the vibration and proceed to part two of their plan.

Seconds later Grimaldi stopped with a jerk and grabbed Stevenson's arm. "Hey, bitch, are you trying to steal my wallet?" he cried.

She responded with a litany of profane Spanish as she tried to pull away.

"Hey, she wants to get paid twice," Chong shouted, and grabbed Stevenson's other arm. He cocked his head toward a nearby alley, and they dragged the screaming woman into the shadows.

The two policemen immediately began to run forward. Bolan raced after them, and when he rounded the corner of the alley he was almost on their heels.

The man on the right started to turn and look, but the Executioner's left fist collided with his jaw. The Cuban's momentum carried him forward, and he plunged face-first to the ground. Bolan looked at the other man, who was drawing a pistol from a shoulder holster under his loose-fitting shirt as he turned. Bolan's hand automatically went to his own sidearm, but the second Cuban suddenly lurched forward as Grimaldi tackled him from behind. The pilot followed the policeman to the ground, one hand holding the wrist of his gun hand as he twisted and delivered an elbow strike to the prone man's temple.

Bolan checked his own downed opponent. The guy was out cold. Chong appeared over Grimaldi's shoulder and said, "Man, you guys are good."

"Help us drag them out of sight," Bolan said, patting down the unconscious Cuban for weapons. He removed one Tokarev pistol from the Cuban's belt, as well as an extra magazine and the man's secret police credentials.

Grimaldi did the same and thrust the weapon he retrieved toward Stevenson. "Looks like you two are now armed," he said.

"I wonder what Mr. Hertel's going to say about that?" Stevenson asked with a wide grin.

"What he doesn't know won't hurt him," Bolan said as he and Chong dragged the unconscious man farther down the alley. The soldier stopped when he was sure they were out of sight, and took out his cell phone. "Bind and mask them," he said to Chong.

The FBI special agent leaned forward and pulled a black burlap sack over the first man's head. After tying it with a loose slipknot, he used plastic cuffs to secure the man's wrists. He took out a second burlap bag and moved to Grimaldi's captive.

Bolan punched in the number for Miguel's cell phone and said, "We're ready."

At the other end of the alley two sets of headlights appeared. The vehicles started toward them. As they drew closer, Bolan saw that the first one was a dilapidated pickup truck, vintage 1959 or so. It was trailed by Miguel's '57 Chevy. The pickup slowed to a stop, and two men jumped out and grabbed the first unconscious Cuban. The men swung him upward and let him drop into the bed of the truck with a loud plunking sound.

Bolan watched as they picked up the second policeman, and as they began to swing the body into the truck, the Executioner grabbed one man by the upper arm.

"Go easy," he said.

He was met by a hostile stare from the Cuba Libre man.

Miguel sauntered forward and spoke quietly in Spanish. Then he looked at Bolan and grinned. "I tell him you are one mean *hombre*, amigo," he said. "But that you no like, how you say, unnecessary violence."

"I heard you," Bolan said. "And these men may be secret

police, but just because they're on the other side doesn't mean they've done something to merit mistreatment. I don't want them harmed."

"Oh, *sí, sí*," Miguel said, then barked quick orders for the second man to be placed more carefully into the truck. "I am sure," he added with a more than a touch of sarcasm, "they would have given us the same humane treatment had things been reversed." He laughed.

"We're not here to kill people," Bolan said. "Unless we have to."

Miguel shot him a half smile, and they watched as the Cubans covered the unconscious policemen with a tarp and placed some bags of sugar on top of them.

Miguel nodded to the two men, who got back into the pickup. The gears ground for several seconds before catching, then the vehicle moved forward. Miguel, a half grin still plastered across his face, motioned toward his Chevy. "Ready?"

The Executioner nodded and they headed for the car. Bolan and Grimaldi got in back, leaving Chong and Stevenson in the front beside Miguel. Stevenson slouched down as much as she could, making her smaller form almost invisible. Miguel shifted into gear and drove out of the alley.

The line of waterfront taverns was fairly deserted as he made his first drive-by. Bolan scanned the area and immediately picked out the bar that was packed with North Korean sailors. He leaned forward and touched Stevenson's shoulder. She felt tense.

"You ready for this?" he asked.

"You bet."

Brave girl, he thought. He was sure neither she nor Chong had much experience in the field, and certainly neither had been expecting to be thrust into the middle of an international operation. He hoped they were fast learners.

"You haven't commented on my new haircut," Chong said, grinning.

"Some things are better left unsaid," Bolan replied, allowing himself a rare moment of levity. "How about you? You ready, as well?"

"Just let me at 'em, boss," Chong said, the smile still on his face. But Bolan detected a bit of nervousness in his tone.

Fast learners, he thought again. Let's hope for a bit of luck, too.

8

La Mesa Gusta
Havana, Cuba

Bolan and Miguel had just dropped off Chong and Stevenson in an alley behind the bars and set up in the Chevy when Miguel got a call on his cell phone.

"My men watching the ship tell me two Korean hombres came down the gangplank in a hurry," he reported. "They're heading for the bars."

Bolan considered that. Were they simply latecomers to the revelry, or was it something else? Perhaps the captain had received orders to shove off earlier than planned, and wanted his crew back in decent shape. Bolan also had to factor in the possibility that the Cuban secret police were starting to search for the missing surveillance team. He picked up his burner phone and called Grimaldi, who answered, "What's up?"

"Looks like a couple newcomers heading your way from the ship," Bolan said. "How's it going in there?"

"Stevenson's already pegged a reasonable facsimile to

Chong. We're waiting for her to prime him a little more and escort him out the back door for a little fun."

Once the unsuspecting and semi-intoxicated North Korean sailor was out of the sight and reach of his companions, the plan was to incapacitate the man and steal his clothes. Chong would then slip onto the ship using distraction number one, plant the transponder, signal he was ready and then slip off again with distraction number two. That was the tricky part, given the FBI agent's inexperience, but the kid was certain he could do it. It was a complex plan, and the Executioner knew those were the worst kind. He reviewed the intricacies once again, and renewed his hope that both Stevenson and Chong were the fast learners they seemed to be.

Miguel was speaking quietly into his cell phone. He turned to Bolan again.

"The two newbies are going to the bars, but they no look like they thinking about having fun."

Bolan nodded and relayed the information to Grimaldi. "They might be en route to herd everybody back to their ship. Better try to speed things up."

"Roger that," Grimaldi said. "I'll meander in and give her a heads-up."

"Be discreet," Bolan said. "We don't want to blow her cover."

"Roger."

Bolan figured he had at least five minutes, and decided to check in with Brognola. He took out his sat phone and punched in the big Fed's number.

"Hey, I was just thinking about calling you," Brognola said. "You want the good news or the bad news?"

"Better give me both."

"Okay. The good news is we located one of those North Korean ships that took off from Mexico four days ago. And the navy was able to set an intercept course. The USS *Rea-*

gan had that contingent of SEALs ready to go, and they were able to board the ship."

"And?" Bolan asked.

"That was the good news. The bad is that they found zilch. Just a lot of bags of sugar, bananas and other assorted junk. No missiles."

"What did the North Koreans say about that?"

"The captain threw a hissy fit, but we didn't pay much attention. The President said we're to take whatever steps necessary to locate and seize those missiles that were illegally removed from that warehouse in Panama."

"So this turned out to be strike one."

"In a manner of speaking. Pyongyang has been uncharacteristically silent on the police action. We were expecting North Korea to threaten to launch a nuke at us."

"Which they'll be able to do soon if they get that technology," Bolan said.

Brognola sighed. "All too true, which is why we have to make sure we target the right boat next time. Speaking of which, how goes that little venture down your way?"

"We're trying to iron out a few wrinkles. I'll let you know soon."

"Okay," Brognola said. "Keep me in the loop"

As Bolan ended the call, he felt his burner phone vibrate in his pocket. He glanced at the screen and saw it was Grimaldi.

"Operation sailor switch is under way," Grimaldi said. "Want to swing by and pick up the trash?"

"I'll send Miguel's guys," Bolan said. "I want to stay here and watch Teresa."

"All right. She and Chong are on their way."

"Is the other guy out?"

"Yep. Down for the count. She slipped him a mickey."

Bolan told Miguel to have his two men in the truck swing down the alley and pick up Grimaldi and the incapacitated North Korean sailor. The Executioner then picked up his night-vision binoculars and zeroed the range finder on the front of the bar. The street was dimly lit, and he saw the two men from the ship Miguel had described approaching the busy establishment.

Stevenson and Chong stumbled out the front door. His gait was exaggerated, and she appeared to be holding him up, helping him walk. From this distance, the kid looked to be turning in an award-winning performance as the proverbial drunken sailor.

The two men from the boat shouted something at the staggering pair, and Chong, his head hanging, lifted his arm in a half-assed salute. The two men kept walking toward the bar. Bolan saw Chong glance over his shoulder, and his movements became crisper and more purposeful.

It looked as if he was trying to speed things up. They were about fifty yards from the dock and the gangplank. Bolan turned to Miguel. "Are your guys ready?"

"Sí," the Cuban said. "One collapsed building coming up."

"Tell them to wait for my signal," Bolan said. He went back to watching through the binoculars. Chong and Stevenson were on a direct course for the gangplank leading to the North Korean freighter and the guard at his post on the dock. This was perhaps the most difficult part of a mission: watching someone else performing a crucial task. The Executioner was used to leading men, but almost always through example. This time, he was relegated to the sidelines while his two inexperienced charges were tasked with performing the subterfuge.

When they were about twenty-five feet away, Bolan saw the gangplank guard's mouth move. He was obviously uttering some kind of command or order. Chong, his head still drooping, again lifted his arm in a mock salute.

"Tell your guys to get ready," Bolan said.

Miguel grunted some instructions into his cell phone.

The gangplank guard stepped forward suddenly, yelling and waving his arms. Chong was hunched over and suddenly leaned forward even more, a spray of dark liquid spewing from his mouth.

Phony vomit, Bolan thought. Nice touch.

The guard jumped backward, away from the spray.

Bolan nodded to Miguel. "Do it."

The Cuban relayed the command, and suddenly an abandoned building on the waterfront crackled, emitted several booms as loud as thunder and began to crumble inward.

To everyone local it would appear to be just another collapse, but it gave Chong the diversion he needed. As the gangplank guard looked at the imploding building about fifty yards away, Chong slipped by him and started up the gangplank. When he was halfway up, a group of four pretty Cuban women, accompanied by two smartly dressed sailors—the ship's officers, no doubt—appeared at the top of the walkway. The women were laughing and swaying their hips. The men with them seemed fully fixated on them, and almost oblivious to the intoxicated sailor ascending the plank. At least that was what Bolan hoped. He nudged the butt of the Tokarev with his elbow, ready to initiate a rescue assault if Chong was discovered.

But the women and officers slipped past Chong, who had turned and leaned over the chain railing with a fake case of dry heaves.

Bolan felt a surge of satisfaction. Part one complete. All the kid had to do now was to find an appropriate place to plant the transponder and then signal he was ready for extrication. Everything was going according to plan so far.

But the Executioner couldn't shake the feeling that something bad was about to happen…

And then he saw it: a big black Soviet-style limou-

sine pulling onto the dock. It raced toward the gangplank
and stopped with a screech. Six men in black BDUs exited the limo carrying long bags that looked as if they
could contain weapons. These guys had the look of professional soldiers… An elite branch. It was doubtful they
were bringing fishing gear on board. The gangplank guard
snapped to attention.

Part two of the plan was in jeopardy.

Punta de las Sueños
Culiacán, Sinaloa, Mexico

YI SAT IN the wooden chair and watched as the Dragon,
shirtless and barefoot, went through his kata on the sandy
beach outside their plush room. The call from Lieutenant
Yoon was overdue, and Yi hoped that did not mean something had gone wrong in Cuba.

The Iranian sat beside Yi, the suitcase filled with money
next to him. He seemed to never let it out of his sight, even
when he would unroll his rug on the floor and do his ritu-
alistic prayers. As a dedicated Communist, Yi had no use
for religion, but did appreciate the Iranian's discipline.
The man never touched alcohol and was totally focused
on the mission. But still, Yi did not fully trust these religious fanatics. He knew they had a selfish reason for helping his country gain access to the nuclear technology and
possession of the old Soviet missiles. The Russians had
promised to help them in updating the long-range capabilities for their ICBMs. Soon the Americans' world domi-
nance would be over, when they were threatened from two
nuclear-armed enemies in opposite hemispheres.

The enemy of my enemy, Yi thought.

The Dragon did a double roundhouse kick, jumped in
the air and performed another snapping front kick.

Yi allowed himself the luxury of one more American

cigarette, which he reached for as he glanced at his watch. It had been over two hours since his conversation with Lieutenant Yoon. He most certainly had to have arrived at the ship and gotten that incompetent captain squared away. Yi considered that perhaps he had erred in assigning Yoon to the task. But the lieutenant had shown aptitude and ability during secret operations in the past, and there was no way Yi wanted to risk sending the Dragon on another assignment so far away.

His sat phone rang just as he placed the cigarette between his lips. He flicked the lighter and lit it before answering. He assumed it was Yoon, and he was correct, but the lieutenant sounded agitated, out of breath, anxious.

"What is happening?" Yi demanded. "Are you on board the ship?"

"Yes, sir," Yoon said. "I have sent two of my men and the ship's officers to collect the remaining members of the crew so that we might disembark as soon as possible."

Yi sensed something more. "What else has gone wrong?"

"We have captured a spy, Colonel."

"A spy?" Yi let the word linger as he ran down the possible ramifications of this development. "Is he Cuban?"

"No," Yoon said, "Korean. But I can tell from his accent that he is not from the South. He sounds like an American."

Yi said nothing. So the Americans were closer than he had anticipated. This was perhaps bad, and perhaps good, depending on how the rest of the game unfolded. And how much they knew.

Yi became cognizant that the Iranian, Basir Farrokhzad, seemed particularly interested in the conversation. He was impetuous enough to lay his hand on Yi's arm and inquire if all was well.

"Just some minor problems," Yi said in English.

The Iranian nodded and smiled politely. "If I may, I should like to speak with my colleague, Amir."

Yi knew he was hardly in a position to refuse the request, since full cooperation of the Iranians was an intricate part of the overall plan. He nodded to Farrokhzad and told Yoon to put the other Iranian on the phone. He then handed the instrument over and listened to the foreign tongue waggling before him. Yi thought about telling the man to speak in English, but decided not to. What could the two of them be talking about that would interfere with the overall mission? And this would build a bit more trust between Yi and the Iranians. He drew some smoke into his lungs, then exhaled.

After what seemed to be more than two minutes Yi began to lose patience. He held up his hand and snapped his fingers.

The Iranian nodded and continued to talk.

Yi thought about making the Iranian pay dearly for his incivility, but instead jumped to his feet and firmly removed the sat phone by bending the man's thumb back with a small pain-compliance grip that assured instant cooperation but no lasting injury.

He put the phone to his ear.

"Basir?" a voice said, followed by something incomprehensible.

"Give the phone back to Lieutenant Yoon," Yi said in English.

"Yes, but of course," the voice replied, also in English.

The Iranian sat in the beach chair massaging his thumb, a look of fear and trepidation in his eyes.

That pleased Yi.

"What are you orders, sir?" Yoon asked.

"Disengage from the harbor as soon as possible," Yi said. "Proceed to the island and have the new missiles loaded. And find out who that spy is and what his superiors know. Report back to me as soon as you have something. Understood?"

"Yes, sir."

Yi could hear the intimidation and fear in Yoon's voice.

Deception, fear and intimidation, Yi thought. All good allies for a leader of men, for a general.

Not that I am a general yet, he thought as he drew heavily on the cigarette, but soon…soon I will be.

Near the harbor
Havana, Cuba

THIS WAS TAKING too long, Bolan thought as he and Miguel sat in the black sedan that the Cuba Libre had "liberated" from the custody of two policemen earlier that night. Something had to have gone wrong. Stevenson, who was seated in the back, seemed to sense Bolan's uneasiness.

"It's not looking good, is it?" she asked.

"It's too early to tell for sure," Bolan said. "But I'm thinking along those lines."

"Oh, God," she said. "What are we going to do now?"

Immediately, Bolan regretted the absence of a good backup plan, but circumstances had dictated that their options for getting Chong off the North Korean ship were limited at best. He mentally reviewed the schematics of the ship that Brognola had emailed to him hours ago, and wondered exactly where the agent might be. The kid's failure to signal that he'd planted the transponder and was ready for the extraction was troubling. So was the sudden and unexpected arrival of what looked to be some special ops North Koreans. Bolan thought back to the firefight at the warehouse and the guy in black BDUs who'd blown up the plane. If these guys were cut from the same cloth, this could spell real trouble.

"Let's go up there," he said to Miguel.

"Go up there? Is your man ready for a pickup?"

"I don't know," Bolan said. "He hasn't signaled yet, but he's been on board way too long. Plus it looks like they're herding the rest of the crew back onto the ship. They may be getting ready to disembark."

If Chong wasn't extracted before that, the situation would go from bad to worse very quickly. Bolan turned to Stevenson. "You ready?"

She nodded.

"Okay," Miguel said, shifting the sedan into gear with a grin. "Let's go play *policías*."

As they turned onto the dock and proceeded toward the ship, Bolan saw two of the North Koreans in BDUs directing a crowd of other reluctant-looking sailors toward the gangplank.

No doubt about it, he thought. They're getting ready to shove off.

Miguel drove around them and pulled up by the gangplank. He opened the driver's door and stepped out with a swagger, tracing his thumb and index finger over the hairs of his thick mustache.

Bolan got out of the vehicle, too, knowing that Grimaldi and the other Cuba Libre men, who were positioned on a rooftop near the entrance to the harbor, would be able to give Miguel and him advanced warning if the real police showed up. He opened the door for Stevenson, who got out and staggered to the front fender.

"I must speak to the captain," Miguel said in Spanish. "There is a problem with one of the men."

The gangplank guard's face twisted into a snarl and he said, *"Aniya. Ka!"*

Bolan knew enough Korean to know that they weren't being welcomed with open arms.

"I must speak with the captain," Miguel repeated, affecting a bit of a swagger.

The guard stood at stoic attention, saying nothing.

Miguel again repeated his request to speak with the captain, and then added, "Do you speak Spanish?"

"He does not speak Spanish," a tall Asian man clad in BDUs said in passable Spanish from the top of the gangplank. "Who are you?"

"We are from the national police," Miguel said. "We have come to investigate a crime that was committed by one of your men a short time ago." He smiled and affected an amiable shrug. "A small matter of nonpayment for services rendered to him by this young woman."

Taking the cue, Stevenson began a harsh litany in Spanish, cursing the malevolent, cheap sailor who hadn't paid her.

"We have no such person on board," the man in black said. "And who is this whore to make such a charge?"

Bolan was impressed with the Korean's Spanish, although it was a bit halting and grammatically imprecise. This guy had definitely been schooled in multiple languages, which most likely meant he was handpicked special forces.

"If this matter is not resolved," Miguel said, "it becomes something more serious. Such as a charge of sexual assault." He paused and lifted his eyebrows. "She can identify the man. Must I remind you that you are guests in my country? You must respect our citizens and our laws."

Bolan felt his burner phone vibrate and ring.

Was it Chong signaling that he was all right and ready to be "taken into custody"?

Keeping up the act, the Executioner extracted the phone from his pocket and answered, *"¿Bueno?"*

"Bueno, my ass," Grimaldi said. "You guys better beat feet outta there. There's a car that looks like the real cops heading your way, and some of those black BDU guys

are mounting what looks like a North Korean M-60 on the fantail."

Bolan terminated the call and smacked Miguel on the arm. "Let's go," he said, and pushed Stevenson toward the sedan.

It was definitely time to get out of there.

9

Punta de las Sueños
Culiacán, Sinaloa, Mexico

James Hudson lay back on the bed in his hotel room with the drink Soo-Han had fixed for him. He still felt unable to relax, despite the attention she was giving him. Finally, he told her to stop, and she looked up at him.

"What is wrong, Jimmy?"

He shook his head. "I'm just feeling the pressure, is all." Reaching down, he took her hand in his and asked, "Soo-Han, does Colonel Yi intend to betray me?"

Her dark eyes widened. "What? Of course not. I would not let him."

That reassured him a bit. Should he tell her about his insurance policy? Perhaps learning that there was one in place would make the colonel a bit more respectful and cautious?

"The party on the beach is close," she said. "Soon you will be rich beyond your wildest dreams, and you will have me, as well."

Hudson smiled. Although he wanted more than anything to believe her, there was a trace of the inscrutable lurking behind those dark eyes. "That's what I wanted to hear. But there's something you should know."

Her eyes narrowed again. "What is that?"

Hudson took a sip of his drink and licked his lips. "I've got the plans from NIISA for the reentry technology downloaded to a flash drive."

She nodded, saying nothing.

He debated telling her more, but thought better of it. At least for now. "I'm going to hold on to it until after he's paid me and we've gotten away."

Kim's eyes darted to the side, then she smiled. "You do not trust Colonel Yi to pay you?"

"Call it a bit of insurance," Hudson said.

"And where is this flash drive?"

He smiled. "If I told you, then it wouldn't be a secret, would it?"

"You don't trust me?" she asked, pouting. "After all we have done together?"

"I trust you, but I can't take the chance he'd hurt you to find out."

She stroked the side of Hudson's face, her soft touch starting to arouse him. "Jimmy," she whispered softly. "I love you."

"I know," he said, pulling her close. "And I love you, too. Just follow my lead and I'll get us through this."

He felt her body move up next to his and he set the drink down on the table beside the bed. Just as he started to kiss her a thudding knock sounded on the door. It seemed anything but polite. She stiffened and looked at him.

"Who's there?" Hudson yelled.

The knock repeated, then he heard the sound of a key being inserted into the lock, the door opening.

Hudson rolled over, using the sheet to cover his nakedness, and reached for the phone. As he picked it up, a Mexican in a cream-colored suit appeared in the doorway, flanked by three other men, all of whom wore loose-fitting black outfits.

"Get the hell out of my room," Hudson said, mustering all the authority a naked, defenseless man caught in bed could muster.

The Mexican raised an eyebrow and flashed a lascivious grin. "Looks like I am interrupting something," he said.

"Who the hell are you and what do you want?" Hudson said, the phone still poised in his hand.

The Mexican pointed at the device and shook his head. "You don't want to do that, amigo."

As if to punctuate the sentence, one of the men in black held open his shirt to reveal the handle of a pistol tucked into his waistband. His other hand held a cylindrical, metallic object that Hudson assumed was a sound suppressor.

"Ricardo is very good at shooting people who give me problems," the Mexican said. "And I'm sure you don't want to give me problems, eh?" He raised his eyebrow again. "All I want is my money, and my man."

They're from the cartel, Hudson thought. And it looks like Yi tried to stiff them, too.

And now there was going to be hell to pay.

Havana, Cuba

BOLAN, STEVENSON AND Miguel had ditched the old Soviet sedan in the abandoned building where they met Grimaldi and another Cuba Libre member. They piled into a pickup truck. Grimaldi and the Cuba Libre man sat in the rear as they sped along the city streets and down several alleys. Miguel's eyes kept darting to the rearview mirror. After about twenty minutes, he shook his head and grinned.

"Looks good so far," he said. "Nobody following us. Where you wanna go now?"

"We've got to regroup," Bolan said. "We have to assume that Chong got caught. We have to get him off that ship. Pull over. I need to make a call."

Miguel nodded and slowed to a stop. He shut off the lights, opened the door and gazed skyward. "They bring the helicopter patrols out after midnight, but most of the time they look for the Libre boats on the water."

Bolan took out his sat phone, already afraid of what he was going to hear, but he knew he had to try, regardless. He called Brognola.

"We've got a problem." He gave the big Fed a quick sitrep.

"Damn," Brognola said. "That doesn't sound good."

"We've got to do a boarding and extract him. Any chance we could get a SEAL team or some Force Recon marines from Gitmo to give us a hand?"

"I'll make some calls to see what I can do." Brognola sighed. "But you know the official stance on independent operatives who run into trouble. I wouldn't count on anything."

The old catchphrase of the government "disavowing all knowledge" played in Bolan's memory like the refrain from an old, sad song, one he'd heard often enough. But it was one thing going into an op being fully aware of the consequences. This time it was a green kid.

And I sent him in there, Bolan thought.

"Let me make those calls and I'll get back to you," Brognola said.

"Roger that," the Executioner replied, knowing that any rescue was now up to him and any limited resources he could find. Even if the President okayed a special ops mission, it would take time. Nothing got decided in Washington without endless hours of discussion, second-guessing and debate.

Someone tapped on the rear window of the truck, and

Bolan turned to see the Cuba Libre man holding up his cell phone and pointing to it. Miguel slid out of the cab and spoke to him. Bolan heard a murmur of quick conversation, and then Miguel reappeared.

"More problems," he said. "My brothers at the harbor say that the North Korean ship has left the port."

Bolan clenched his teeth. Things were going from bad to worse in a hurry.

"You said something before about having access to a speedboat?" Bolan asked.

"Sí."

"How far is it?"

Miguel shrugged. "Roughly thirty minutes away."

Thirty minutes. It was their best shot for intercepting the North Koreans. At this point, it was their only shot.

"Let's go for it," Bolan said.

10

Punta de las Sueños
Culiacán, Sinaloa, Mexico

The bar was deserted except for the three of them. The Mexican in the cream-colored suit, who was now identifying himself as Jose, sprawled in the rear of the booth sipping tequila. Hudson sat next to him, feeling pale, weak and inadequate. He hadn't touched the glass of liquid before him, and was conscious of one of the men in black sitting a few tables away, watching them. The other two had stayed in the room with Kim, while Hudson called Yi and told him they had to meet in the bar immediately. The colonel walked in, accompanied by the Dragon, and strode to Hudson. He stopped when he saw Jose, and then casually glanced over to the man in black.

"I see you have brought a friend," Yi said. He motioned for Hudson to slide over and allow him to sit. The Dragon remained standing.

"Buenas noches, señor," Jose said. "I see you have brought your, ah, bodyguard with you. You want some

tequila?" He brought the glass to his lips and tossed down its contents.

Yi watched with no curiosity or interest.

The Mexican slammed the glass onto the table and poured himself another drink. His lips curled into a smile as he nodded toward the Dragon. "Why don't you tell your dog to sit?"

Yi gazed at the man as if assessing him, and said something in Korean. The Dragon slowly walked over to the man in black and sat opposite him. The two bodyguards stared at each other over the tabletop like two big jungle cats sizing each other up.

Jose picked up the glass again, rotating it between his fingers. "My friend, it has been long time since we last talked. And almost as long since I heard from Roberto, the man I sent to meet you in Panama." He paused, belched and continued. "You see, my friends down in Panama City tell me that they have not heard from their man, Paco, either. They fear for his health. What can you tell me about that?"

Yi sat impassively, saying nothing.

"We don't want trouble," Jose said. "We just want our money, like we agreed. But if it's trouble you want, we can give you plenty." He brought the glass to his lips and drank.

"Your man is on my boat," Yi said. "He wished to remain there to guard the money that the Iranians brought. I complied with his wish."

Jose smirked. "At one time, I might have believed you, but I know Paco. He is my cousin. He would not make such a decision without first calling me."

"We thought it best to maintain strict communication silence," Yi said. "But if you are worried, I will have him contact you. Tomorrow. The hour grows late here, and I need my rest."

Jose's smile twisted into a snarl. "I don't think so. I think you will call him now. Pronto. I want to talk to him."

Hudson didn't like the way this was shaping up. It was like being between two bulls getting ready to butt heads.

"You would be wise to keep your manners about you," Yi said.

"And you would be wise to remember you are in my backyard." Jose motioned to the man in black, who stood and began to reach inside his shirt.

In a flash, the Dragon was on his feet and delivering a quick backhanded blow to his temple. The man in black crumpled to the table, and the Dragon moved behind him, his forearm snaking around his neck. He gripped the man's collar with his left hand and made a quick twisting motion with his right. The cartel man's head flopped to one side, his body going in the opposite direction. The man's eyes took on a glazed look as the Dragon repositioned him in the chair, removing his pistol as he did so. Jose's jaw dropped and Yi lurched forward, grabbing the Mexican by the throat, his fingers digging into his flesh, causing him to make a gurgling sound as his eyes bulged in their sockets.

"You would do well to remember that one should not consume alcohol during an important meeting," Yi said calmly. "Not only is it not polite, but it dulls one's senses."

Jose continued to gurgle, he face turning an uneven shade of scarlet.

"See if he is armed," Yi said to Hudson, who complied immediately.

When Hudson had finished the pat down he said, "He's clean, but there are two more men in my room with Soo-Han. They forced their way in. I'm sure they're armed. He's probably got more around here, too."

Yi frowned. "I seem to have underestimated these Mexican gangsters. It is a mistake I must seek to rectify now." He released the gasping Jose, who fell forward, his forehead bouncing off the tabletop. Yi nodded to the Dragon.

"Let the reckoning begin," Yi said.

On the beach
Havana, Cuba

THE FOUR OF THEM, Bolan, Grimaldi, Miguel and the second Cuba Libre man, Delmar, needed the illumination from the truck's headlights to negotiate the treacherous walk through the thick underbrush down to the water. Once they got on the sandy beach, Bolan had them halt and set the boat down. He turned and was about to signal Stevenson to shut off the truck's headlights when he heard the sound of an approaching chopper.

Miguel's head shot up. "Police helicopter," he said.

Bolan nodded.

"Leave the boat," Miguel said. "They must not catch us."

The speedboat had been their one chance to catch the North Korean ship, but now that opportunity seemed negated. Still, failure was not an option.

"How many men do they usually have on those helicopter patrols?" Bolan asked.

Miguel shrugged. "Two. Sometimes four." He glanced around quickly. "Tell *la señorita* to close off the lights of the truck before they see us."

Bolan glanced up at the black velvet sky. The lights of the helicopter were coming closer. He made no signal to Stevenson. Instead, a new idea came to him.

"Jack, find some cover in the shrubbery. When they land, take out the pilot."

Grimaldi grinned. "Am I thinking what you're thinking?"

Bolan nodded. "Probably."

"Hot damn! Things are looking up."

"What are you planning?" Miguel asked.

Bolan knew that the mindset of Cuba Libre was always to evade rather than confront, which worked well with their covert operations and survival. But being evasive wasn't in the cards if they wanted to rescue Chong.

"We're going to commandeer that helicopter."

Miguel's face showed flabbergasted surprise, and then he grinned. "Okay, amigo. We will follow your lead."

The helicopter was hovering above them now, perhaps at three hundred feet. Bolan pulled out his Tokarev and pointed it at Miguel and Delmar, both of whom now had their hands on their heads. The helicopter circled, its occupants shining a large spotlight on the three of them. The beam swept across the beach toward the still-lit truck.

"Atención, este es la policía nacionale de la revolución. Quede alla."

Bolan held skyward the credentials he'd taken from the policeman earlier, keeping the pistol trained on the two men.

The pilot repeated his warning not to move as the chopper descended, sending a swirl of sand over the trio as it landed on the beach about thirty yards away. Bolan blinked several times to clear his stinging eyes. He hoped Grimaldi had chosen a good position. The helicopter looked like a Russian Mi-24 Hind, with gun mounts and rocket pods. These guys were enforcers, pure and simple. Any Cubans fleeing the island in boats were defenseless target practice.

The side door opened and a man got out, jumping down onto the sand. He strode toward them with a swagger, holding a pistol in his right hand.

"What's going on?" the policeman asked in a gruff voice.

To the rear of the helicopter, a shadow moved across the sand.

Grimaldi.

Bolan waited until the man was about twenty-five feet away and whirled, leveling the pistol at the policeman's chest.

"Detener," Bolan said. *"No se mueva."*

The man brought his own gun upward and the Executioner squeezed the trigger, not going for a kill shot. He watched the Cuban twist and fall to the ground. Bolan felt a momentary pang at shooting a member of a police force, secret or not, but this man was an exterminator whose duty was to stop those innocents fleeing the island. He definitely was not a soldier on the side of right.

Miguel and his partner had flattened themselves on the sand by the time Bolan saw Grimaldi open the door of the chopper and pull out the pilot. The two struggled, silhouetted against the aircraft's lights, for several seconds as Bolan moved forward and stripped the gun out of the fallen policeman's hand, then turned and ran toward them. He had covered perhaps half the distance when a dull crack pierced the night. One of the two shadows stiffened and then slumped to the ground. Bolan slowed and brought his weapon to chest level, acquiring a sight picture on the man who remained standing.

The shadow shrugged and turned to face him, offering a better target.

"If you're going to shoot me, you'd better plan on someone else flying this bird," Grimaldi said.

Bolan lowered the Tokorev and smiled. That was Jack, always ready with a wisecrack even when somebody was pointing a gun at him.

Punta de las Sueños
Culiacán, Sinaloa, Mexico

YI KEPT A come-along hold on Jose's left arm as they marched him up to Hudson's room. The Dragon gripped the man's right arm in similar fashion. Hudson trailed behind the procession. The Dragon held the dead Mexican's pistol with the sound suppressor down by his right leg as they walked. Thankfully, at this late hour the hallways of the hotel were pretty much deserted. Yi stopped at the corner leading to Hudson's room and said something to the Dragon, who nodded. The colonel took out his cell phone and pressed a few buttons, again speaking in Korean, issuing a few harsh-sounding orders and then clicking off.

"What's going on?" Hudson asked.

Yi regarded him coldly, saying nothing.

"Listen," Hudson said, "you'd better tell me the plan if you want me to help you resolve this mess."

Yi was still silent.

Hudson tried to suppress his anger.

The prick's acting like it's all my fault, he thought. Like I'm responsible for him shortchanging his partners. Hudson licked his lips in frustration and started to speak again, but Yi held up his palm in a silencing gesture. For a moment Hudson thought the man was going to hit him, but he didn't.

"You have shown yourself to be little more than a coward," Yi said. "You allowed me to be led into a trap when you summoned me to the bar. This I will not forget."

"They had a gun to my head," Hudson said. "Plus they were threatening Soo-Han. What else could I do?"

Yi let out a short, quick burst of air, a snort of pure derision. "You could have shown some courage," he said. "The warrior's code. Even this gangster has shown me more resolve than you have." Yi glanced at Jose and tightened the arm lock, causing the other man to grunt in pain. "Do not think I have forgotten about you. Now, tell me again how many more men you have spread out throughout this hotel."

"Just the two inside the room," the Mexican grunted. "That's all."

Yi gritted his teeth, obviously increasing the pressure

on the gangster's left arm. "Do you take me for a fool? How many?"

Jose's lips twisted open in a grimace of pain, showing his teeth. "I'm not lying to you."

Yi shifted his weight, ratcheting up the pressure again. "Must I break your wrist before you tell me the truth?"

"Okay, okay," Jose said, the words bursting from his mouth. "There are five more."

"What are their locations?" Yi gritted.

"Two in the lobby," the Mexican said. "Three more out back with our car."

Yi smiled and nodded, but the smile faded in a millisecond, replaced by a stern look that sent a shiver up Hudson's spine.

"If you have lied to me," Yi said, "I guarantee you will pray for death long before it is granted to you."

"I'm telling the truth!"

Yi turned back to Hudson. "It is still not too late to redeem yourself, Jimmy." Hudson knew that Yi was mocking him. "Help us in gaining access to the room, and we will handle the rest."

Hudson was well aware that he was in no position to argue. "Tell me what you want me to do."

Yi nodded and leaned close to Jose, their faces only inches apart. "We are going to the door. You will tell your men inside that you have returned, and to open it." He reached up and gripped the Mexican's face with his free hand, squeezing the man's cheeks together so that his lips puckered. "And remember, we do understand your language. *¿Comprender?*"

Jose nodded, barely able to move his head.

Yi said something to the Dragon, who released Jose's right arm and motioned for Hudson to take his spot at the gangster's side. He did so, and they turned the corner and briskly walked down the hallway toward Hudson's room.

The Dragon walked behind them, holding the pistol. When they arrived at the door, Yi positioned Jose in front of the peephole and pulled Hudson close to the gangster's right shoulder. Yi nodded and Hudson knocked three times.

"¿Quién?" a voice said from inside the room.

"Soy yo," Jose said. *"Abra la puerta."*

Some movement was audible there, then some fumbling with the lock. The door opened a crack and a face appeared. Yi shifted his weight, twisting forward and to the left, slamming Jose's head into the partially open door. The Mexican behind the panel tumbled from sight. Hudson was frozen in place as the Dragon drove Jose's body forward, thrusting him into the room, the door swinging back despite the opposition of the pneumatic closing device.

The Dragon shot the first gangster in the head as he struggled to rise from his position by the door. The Mexican dropped instantly and the Dragon brought the pistol up. Two gangsters sat behind the small kitchenette table with Soo-Han. They started to get up, both reaching for their guns. The Dragon fired two shots that caught the first man in the chest. Rotating slightly, he nailed the other in the left eye. That man slumped forward, blood pouring out of his mouth as he flopped onto the tabletop.

Kim stood in the center, between the two dead bodies, the translucent white material of her robe, as well as her bare shoulders, dappled with specks of red blood. The Dragon inspected each man and then turned and said something to Yi in Korean.

The colonel nodded. He still had Jose in an arm lock and now forced the Mexican to his knees. Yi raised his right arm and delivered three sharp chops to the other man's exposed side. Jose grunted in pain with each one and curled into a ball.

The colonel stood, took out his cell phone and punched

in a number. Seconds later he issued several commands in Korean.

Hudson ran over to Soo-Han and tried to embrace her. She pushed him away with a look of disgust on her face. Yi uttered something, and Kim's expression softened into a smile.

"Please, Jimmy," she said. "I must clean myself."

Hudson stepped back and nodded. "Sorry," he said.

She walked toward the bathroom.

Things had gone from bad to worse, Hudson thought. But at least she was safe. For the moment. He felt Yi's hand on his shoulder. The man's grip was anything but cordial.

"I have instructed the other Black Tigers to sweep the building and the grounds," he said. "The other gangsters will be dealt with."

"That's good to know," Hudson said. He wanted them all to get the hell out of his room. He wanted to hold Soo-Han. He wanted to make sure she was all right.

"We must not let this unexpected intrusion affect our overall plan." Yi stroked his jaw with his fingers. "An intelligent general must be able to turn a complication into an advantage."

Hudson nodded, wondering what in the hell Yi was talking about.

"We must accelerate our timeline," the colonel said. "We take them tonight. Now."

"Take who?" Hudson said. He didn't like the way this was unraveling.

"Turner and Nabokovski," Yi said. "We cannot afford to wait for the possibility of another attack."

"Okay." Hudson rubbed his temples. "What about my money?"

Yi frowned. "You will give me the computer attachment with the information now."

Hudson was stunned. How the hell had Yi found out

about the flash drive? Was the room bugged? Another thought chilled him: Soo-Han. Had she betrayed him? Told Yi everything? Hudson tried to subdue the sickening feeling in his stomach and said, "Listen, I want my money now."

Yi shook his head, his face showing a trace of irritation. "When I have that computer attachment and the two scientists and I are safely away from here, you will get your reward."

Hudson licked his lips, then nodded. He didn't like the sound of that, but what choice did he have at this point?

Besides, he thought, I still have my little insurance policy. The passwords to unlock the encryptions were on his laptop, which was still locked in the room safe. Even Soo-Han didn't know the combination for that one.

Over the Florida Straits
Near Cuba

As GRIMALDI PILOTED the helicopter on an intercept course with the North Korean ship, Bolan, who was in the copilot's seat, thought about his recent conversation with Brognola.

"The good news is that the transponder the kid managed to plant is working fine," the big Fed had said. "We've got a fix on the location of the freighter."

"Let me guess," Bolan had said. "It's headed out of the harbor and toward an island hideaway near Camarioca."

"You got it." Brognola sighed. "The President's in conference with his team of advisers trying to figure out our next move, but…"

Bolan knew full well what that meant: they were on their own, as far as a rescue attempt was concerned. He didn't waste any more time discussing it. "See if you can get our navy to keep the light on for us at the Naval Air Station, Key West."

Brognola was silent for several seconds, then said, "Roger that. Good luck, Striker."

Stevenson, who was seated behind Bolan, handed him another magazine for the Tokarev and he made sure it was at full capacity. He nodded and placed the extra mag into the lower left-side pocket of his cargo pants.

Grimaldi pointed to the radar screen. "There she is. Keep in mind we've got about fifteen minutes max to wrap this up, if we want to save enough fuel to get home."

Bolan nodded. "I'll keep that in mind, but regardless, every minute Chong's held prisoner down there is one too many."

Grimaldi nodded. "I hear ya."

Stevenson, who didn't have earphones on, shouted her question at Bolan. "What did he say?"

The soldier leaned close to her ear. "That fortune favors the bold. Now get ready to switch places. I'm going to tie off."

She nodded and stood in a crouch. The confines of the helicopter were so tight that even she had to stoop a bit. Bolan removed his earphones, placed them on Stevenson's head and slid out of the front seat. He checked the knot and snugness of the Swiss seat he'd tied around his waist and legs and then clipped the D ring in place. Next he adjusted the straps of the backpack with the explosives he'd gotten from Miguel, and checked the security of his Tokarev and ammo.

Through the Plexiglas window, the water below looked almost black. Bolan opened the side door slightly and lashed the nylon cable securely around the cleat, tying it off with a tight square knot. He saw what he knew was the darkened silhouette of the superstructure of the North Korean ship. They were running without lights. He flipped down the night-vision goggles.

Bolan tapped Grimaldi's shoulder twice and moved to the door. Stevenson glanced over her shoulder and the Executioner nodded, giving her a thumbs-up. She smiled weakly and did the same. He pulled the side door all the way open and held the coiled line in his hand.

"Atención, atención," Stevenson said, using the helicopter's public-address system. *"Somos la policía naciónal de la revolución de Cuba. Tienen que presentar sus identificaciónes enseguida."*

She repeated the message as Grimaldi positioned the helicopter directly over the ship, slowly lowering so that it hovered about a hundred feet above the center of the vessel. The freighter was still dark, but Bolan could see movement on the deck with the night-vision goggles. He tossed the nylon cable outward, watching it unravel in the darkness like a nervous serpent, then he positioned himself on the outside skid.

Stevenson repeated the message, and Bolan took one more glance downward through the goggles. The green illumination showed the line was fully extended, and he trusted Grimaldi's judgment at estimating the height. The Executioner extended his body outward so that his head was well below the helicopter's steel rung, and then he pushed, and felt himself falling. The nylon rope slid through his gloved fingers, making a zipping sound in the still night as he whirled downward. He completed his rappel, zooming down between the perpendicular cranes, with only two momentary pauses to slow his descent, and then felt the solidness of the cargo bay coverings beneath his feet.

Bolan unclipped the D ring and drew his pistol. Two men rushed forward, one in black BDUs. Each carried an AK-47. Bolan raised the Tokarev and fired two shots into each man. The one in the BDUs was obviously one of the special forces commandos who'd boarded the ship earlier. How many were actually on board was pure supposition at this point, but Bolan figured on at least five more.

The schematics of the ship that Brognola had emailed to him earlier flashed in Bolan's memory as he advanced toward the bridge. That was where he surmised they were holding Chong. The majority of the vessel was taken up by the hold, for cargo space. The bridge area held crew quarters, the galley and officers' quarters.

A sudden burst of machine-gun fire reverberated in the night and Bolan saw muzzle flashes coming from the bow. The rounds were directed skyward. The helicopter darted away.

Bolan quickened his pace. He passed a metal shunt that curved and opened toward the ship's center.

An air duct for the cargo hold, he thought.

A metal lid secured the duct, allowing it to be opened to admit fresh air, but closed to keep out water in case of a rough sea.

He stopped and crouched nearby, slipping the backpack off his shoulders. The explosives had been equipped with a timer, which Bolan set for fifteen minutes. That would be his alarm clock. Hopefully, he would have enough time to find Chong. He twisted the hatches free, opened the lid of the duct and dropped the knapsack down the metal shoot.

He glanced at his watch, memorizing the time: 0121. At 0136 they'd be getting a nice surprise. Closing the lid, he resumed his trek toward the bridge. Another BDU-clad figure appeared about thirty feet away, carrying a rifle and directing two other Koreans, who looked to be civilian sailors, to fan out. Both of them carried rifles, as well.

Bolan flattened himself against the side wall and waited, his pistol ready. As soon as the three men began to move on, he acquired a sight picture on the BDU-clad figure and fired. The man's hand went to his upper chest and the green image showed a gush of dark-colored blood bursting from his mouth. The other two looked back, and Bolan shot them in turn, aiming for center mass in each instance.

Then he moved on.

The bridge was only about twenty-five yards away now, but it rose several stories. Except for a row of windows across the top level, only a smattering of portholes were located on the side facing him. That most likely meant there wasn't a lot of cabin space. And the bridge had to be on the top floor.

Four sailors stood guard in front of the stairway leading upward. Bolan flattened out next to the last cargo bin cover and ejected the partially depleted magazine for a combat reload. He tossed the expended mag across the deck and watched as the eyes of the four guards focused on the noise. He picked them off, firing from right to left, then followed up by placing a well-aimed shot to each fallen man's head.

Bolan replaced the Tokarev in its holster as he ran to the bodies and stripped the first one of his AK-47, then took the magazines from the other three. Things would be a little more even now. Jamming the extra mags into his belt line, Bolan did a quick check of the rifle, making sure it had a full load and a round in the chamber.

He checked his watch: 0130.

Six minutes to find Chong. He raised the rifle to a ready position and moved to the opposite side of the stairwell. The space was tight, which didn't provide much room for evasion or cover, but conversely, it was open on the side and visibility upward was good.

A flash of movement fluttered above—a pair of legs and the descending barrel of an AK-47, along with an inquiry in Korean.

Bolan's weapon was already pointed upward and he squeezed the trigger. The legs jerked in a spasmodic little dance, and the body of a man in black BDUs fell down the stairway. Bolan paused to sweep the body with a quick burst and stepped over the dead man. One more level and he'd be at the top.

He covered the distance as rapidly as he could, figuring that hardmen would respond to the sound of gunfire. He encountered no one until he got to the uppermost level. Pausing at the corner juncture to take a quick look, Bolan saw a bright flash from what had to have been a handgun as the metal inches from his head rang from the collision of the projectile. The Executioner swiveled the barrel of the AK-47 around the edge of the steel doorway and fired a burst. He pulled back, dropped the near-empty magazine and slammed a new one into place. He checked to make sure the ejection port was still closed, meaning there was still one in the pipe, and stuck the barrel around the corner again, firing off another short burst.

No response.

Firing yet another quick burst, Bolan slid around the corner and advanced quickly, finding himself in an enclosed area resembling a small recreational room. He looked down and saw another fallen BDU-clad body, arm outstretched, pistol lying nearby. Bolan kicked the gun away as he stepped past the dead man. He estimated that he had only a few short minutes to locate Chong before the blast would occur. How much damage it would do was anybody's guess, but he was counting on it as a diversion tactic more than anything else.

The door to the bridge was closed, and Bolan could see a line of light underneath, interrupted by moving shadows. It was a regular wooden door, rather than one of the steel ones he'd seen thus far. It would afford little ballistic protection to anyone on the other side, but the Executioner wasn't sure of any targets within. Chong could be there, and vulnerable. Bolan raised his foot and gave the door a hard kick. It swung open, bouncing off the wall, and started closing again. Three men were inside, two of whom held pistols. Bolan shot one and then the other, skipping over the man in the center who had been standing by the ship's wheel. He appeared to be the captain.

"Where's the American?" Bolan shouted.

"I…not good English," he stuttered, his eyes full of fear.

Bolan pointed the rifle barrel at the captain's face and repeated, "The American."

The man's eyes shot toward a closed door on the other side of the bridge. Bolan strode to the captain, spun him and grabbed him by the neck. They moved toward the door like two ungainly dancers.

"Open it," Bolan said, his voice a growl.

The captain hesitated and Bolan jammed the barrel of the rifle against the man's spine.

"Do it."

The captain tentatively gripped the doorknob and twisted it, then pushed the door open slowly, saying, *"Nahm ne dah. Chung sogee masayo."*

A shot rang out from inside the room and the captain's body stiffened. Bolan glanced inside. Chong was tied to a chair. A man in black BDUs, the one who had spoken to them earlier, crouched behind Chong's shoulder. Another man, dressed in a suit and definitely not Asian, fired a pistol. A round whizzed by Bolan's head, chipping wood off the doorjamb. The Executioner twisted slightly and fired the AK-47 at the man in the suit. He jerked spasmodically as the heavy rifle rounds chewed through him. The crouching man's arm was extended now and he fired his pistol. Bolan kept the captain's body in front of him as he brought up the barrel of the AK-47, reacquired a quick sight picture on the crouching man's head and fired.

Holes appeared in the middle of the man's forehead as the wall in back of him was suddenly decorated with a splattering of crimson. He fell forward, landing on the floor next to the chair. The Executioner quickly cleared the rest of room and checked the status of his assailants. Both were dead.

He ran to Chong. The agent's face was swollen, and his bare upper body was stained with cuts, cigarette burns and smears of blood. His left eye was completely closed, but a bright brown iris darted between the thick lids of his right. Torn lips formed a weak smile, leaving a glaze of blood over white teeth.

"What the hell kept you?" he managed to say.

Bolan withdrew a combat knife from his pocket and cut the ropes that bound the man to the chair. "Can you walk?" he asked.

"I'll try. One of those guys was guarding that suitcase over there."

Bolan strode to the large case. He gave it a quick examination, deciding it was not booby-trapped, and opened it. The suitcase was full of money—euros and US currency. He closed it and rejoined Chong. He helped the agent to his feet and held his arm while he took a few tentative steps.

"I can make it," Chong grunted. "Where to?"

"Up top," Bolan said. "It's the only place we can safely set down, once Jack takes care of a little business."

"Business?"

Before Bolan could answer, a muffled roar reverberated from deep inside the ship. It seemed to shake the vessel for a split second.

Despite the ringing in his ears from the auditory exclusion brought about from the gunfire, Bolan had regained a good portion of his hearing. He took out his cell phone and hit the speed-dial button. Stevenson answered on the first ring.

"We're heading up," Bolan said.

He thought he heard her say okay, but wasn't sure. It didn't matter. Bolan knew Grimaldi would be there for them, come hell or high water.

Bolan grabbed the suitcase, then steered Chong toward the doorway. The FBI agent managed only a few steps before sagging.

"I can't make it after all," he muttered.

Bolan stopped and slung his rifle, holding Chong upright.

"You go on without me," the FBI agent urged.

Without a word Bolan hoisted Chong onto his left shoulder. "Nobody gets left behind." He picked up the suitcase with his other hand.

As the Executioner rounded the corner, he saw a ladder leading to the roof of the bridge area. A sudden burst of heavy rounds exploded across the top of the cabins, and Bolan realized that one of the special forces soldiers manned the fantail machine gun. He dropped to the deck and slid the AK-47 off his shoulder, but before he could fire he saw the helicopter rise about a hundred feet off the right side of the ship. A flash of light rippled from the rocket pod on the helicopter's left side and the fantail exploded in a burst of yellow light. Bolan saw the helicopter cant to the right, seeming to turn on a dime, and another flash puffed from the rocket pod, leaving a trail of white smoke against the velvet backdrop.

Bolan guessed that the machine-gun position on the bow no longer existed.

He got to his feet and shouldered Chong again, leaving the suitcase for a later recovery. "Try to relax. We're almost home free."

11

US Naval Hospital
Naval Air Station, Key West, Florida

Bolan watched as Grimaldi made his way down the hallway carrying two cups of coffee. He stopped in front of the chairs and handed one to Stevenson, then took a sip from the other.

"You didn't want any, right?" he said to Bolan with a quick wink.

The Executioner shook his head and stood. He felt sore, but not tired, most likely due to the lingering adrenaline that was still floating through his system. Standing, he pointed to the suitcase he'd recovered from the North Korean ship and told Grimaldi to keep an eye on it. When the pilot nodded, Bolan took out his sat phone and walked away.

He speed dialed Brognola's number and hit Send. A few rings later, the big Fed picked up. "How's the kid doing?"

"They worked him over pretty good," Bolan said. "He had some internal injuries, but he's got grit. Looks like he'll be all right."

"Outstanding." Brognola sighed. "They were still debating what to do in the situation room when I called to tell them you already got our man back."

"Well, here's something else you need to run by them. Are you having any luck finding those North Korean ships?"

"As a matter of fact, they're closing on one as we speak. Let's hope it's the right one. The North Koreans are already bellowing about some kind of retaliation if we board another one."

"Remember we were wondering who was paying the bills for all this?"

"Yeah," Brognola grunted.

"I think it might be the Iranians. When Chong was being held on the North Korean ship, he feigned being unconscious between beatings. At one point he overheard someone on a sat phone speaking what he's sure was Farsi."

"Makes sense," Brognola said. "The North Koreans don't have a pot to piss in, moneywise. The Iranians could be bankrolling them."

"Plus there was a non-Asian guy, possibly Iranian, in the cabin there. I didn't have time to search him, but I did recover a suitcase full of money. US dollars and euros."

"Interesting."

"So think about it. There's not much doubt that the North Koreans are the prime suspects in stealing those missiles from Panama. They had three ships that left the Canal Zone right after the theft. They had to figure that we'd be tracking those vessels and possibly going to search them."

"Yeah…" Brognola said slowly.

"Suppose the missiles aren't on any of the three North Korean ships that left Mexico." Bolan waited a few beats, then asked, "Were there any Iranian ships that were also there?"

"I see what you're saying." Brognola's voice took on a tone of excitement. "It's a variation of the old shell game. What shell is the peanut under? Answer, none of them."

"That would be my guess."

"I'll get Aaron busy checking on any Iranian ships heading toward the peninsula above the thirty-eighth parallel."

Bolan felt the vibration of an incoming call. He did a quick check of the screen and saw an unfamiliar number.

"I've got another call coming in, Hal," he said. "Let me get back to you."

"A new call?" Brognola sounded flustered. "Who—"

Bolan didn't wait for him to finish, just pressed the button to accept the new call.

"*Buenos días*, my friend," a voice said. "It is Sergeant Martinez."

"Jesus? What's the occasion?"

"Captain Ruiz has broken," Martinez said. "As I told you he would. He has given us significant information about the situation we stumbled into during the raid. And much, much more."

"What did you find out?"

"As we suspected, the cartel had been bribing many officials," Martinez said, "including Ruiz. This latest deal involved two foreign governments, North Korea and Iran. The Asian you killed during the raid must have been Korean."

Bolan said nothing, even though he had already surmised that much.

"Ruiz told us that the bribes were significant," Martinez continued. "And these agents are still in Mexico, in Culiacán. They are meeting with some Americans."

That got Bolan's attention. "Do you know where?"

"They are at a resort called Punta de las Sueños. I have already sent a squad of my best marines there. They wait for me to join them."

"Do you know who the Americans are?"

"At this time, I do not."

Bolan thought about this new wrinkle in the scenario. How did Americans figure into it, if this whole thing was about old Soviet missiles? Obviously, there were more than just a few pieces of the puzzle still missing. He also thought about the firefight on the ship involving the North Korean special forces squad.

"Jesus," Bolan said. "I've already tangled with a few of those North Koreans over here. They're some pretty rough hombres. Special forces from the looks of them. Can you wait until I get there?"

Martinez laughed. "Are you trying to question my ability? Or appeal to *el machismo mexicano*?" He snorted another laugh. "I appreciate the warning, but we cannot afford to wait."

Bolan thought about that and realized he was too far away to make a difference. But he had to get to Culiacán fast.

"Good luck, Jesus," the Executioner said. "You can tell us all about it when we get there. Stay safe."

"*Gracias*, my friend. I will see you later."

Bolan immediately called Brognola back and gave him the update.

"Americans?" the big Fed said.

"We need to get to Culiacán now," Bolan told him. "Can you grease some wheels for us?"

"Leave it to me."

Bolan terminated the call and went back to the waiting area. Grimaldi apparently had Stevenson enthralled with some kind of story. The Executioner beckoned him over and said softly, "I just wanted to let you know we've got to go to Culiacán."

Grimaldi nodded. "Just say when."

After getting more coffee, Bolan explained to Stevenson that he and Grimaldi had to leave.

"I don't how I'm going to be able to write all this up in a report," she said. "At least how to do it so I can keep my job."

"Write it up as it happened," Bolan said. "And as far as keeping your job, don't worry about it. I'll make a few phone calls." He pointed to the suitcase. "Just make sure you take care of that. It's evidence."

Stevenson nodded. "I need to do a count. Can you help me verify it?"

Bolan looked around, then shook his head. "This isn't the time or place. And we'll be leaving soon."

Bolan heard the elevator doors opening behind him. He turned to see two men in short-sleeve khakis step off and begin to walk toward them. One wore a lieutenant's insignia. The other man was a captain.

Both officers stopped in front of Bolan. Although the captain's uniform looked freshly pressed and impeccable, his face showed the stubble of a blue-black beard and more than a trace of fatigue.

"Which one of you is Cooper?" the lieutenant asked.

"I am," Bolan said.

The man turned with deference toward the higher-ranking man.

"I'm Captain Gryczewski," he said. "Base commander."

Bolan nodded.

Gryczewski lifted his eyebrows and took a deep breath. "It's not often I get a call from SecNav at this hour instructing me to get out of bed and loan an F-15 Eagle to a couple of civilians, no less."

"Aw, hell, Captain," Grimaldi said. "It's okay. We're both vets."

Gryczewski paused and shook his head slightly. "All I

can say is you guys must have some clout. Which one of you is the pilot?"

"That would be me," Grimaldi said.

The captain gave him a once-over and asked, "You know how to fly an F-15?"

"As long as it's got wings or rotors," Grimaldi said, "I can fly it."

The captain frowned. "That's reassuring." He sighed. "But I'm not going to argue with SecNav. I've been told to see to this personally, so follow me."

The two naval officers turned and began walking back toward the elevators.

Bolan turned to Stevenson. "Looks like we're leaving sooner rather than later. Goodbye and good luck."

Stevenson smiled sadly. "Despite Henry being almost beaten to death, this was quite the adventure. Keep safe."

"You don't need adventures like this one. Take care," Bolan said as he turned to follow the two naval officers.

Grimaldi gave Stevenson a quick hug and hurried after his old friend.

It was time to head to Culiacán for round two.

Culiacán International Airport
Culiacán, Sinaloa, Mexico

YI WATCHED AS the final pieces of luggage were loaded onto the Iranian's private Learjet. The plane was sleek, and apparently had enough space that they would not be cramped on their flight back to the homeland. He did feel a bit vulnerable leaving his weapons behind at the resort, but the demonstrated skill of the Black Dragon had been more than sufficient to intimidate both the American and the Russian scientists. They seemed resigned to becoming "guests" of North Korea.

The beating the Dragon had administered to Hudson,

after Yi discovered that the computer attachment was encrypted, had served a dual purpose. Not only had it elicited the location of the deciphering codes, Hudson's laptop, but it had also shown the two scientists that any resistance or lack of cooperation would make them the next targets. Neither man appeared to be much of a fighter.

The Iranian, Basir Farrokhzad, approached Yi and placed a tentative hand on the colonel's shoulder. Yi turned and regarded him.

"We must be going," Farrokhzad said. "We are cleared for departure."

Yi shook his head. "We will not leave until Soo-Han returns with Hudson's laptop." He glanced at his watch with a bit of concern. They had been gone over an hour. Perhaps a call was in order. He took out his cell phone and punched in Kim Soo-Han's number. It rang several times and then went to voice mail.

"Colonel," Farrokhzad said, his voice pleading now. "We know that the Americans have discovered some, perhaps all, of our plot. Remember, my compatriot in Cuba called hours ago to tell me that they were raiding the ship. I have not been able to reach him since. We must leave."

Yi listened to Kim's recorded voice advising that she was not available and to leave a message.

"They might be sending their jets to shoot us down," the Iranian continued.

"They would not dare," Yi said. "The Americans are paper tigers."

"Please. We must leave now."

Yi glanced at his watch again. "Five minutes more, and then we go."

He had dispatched Soo-Han and three Black Tigers back to the resort to recover Hudson's laptop. If they had encountered problems, he could rely on her to find her own way back to the homeland. And with the two scientists and the computer attachment in hand, his return would still appear to be a success. As far as the encryption of the files went, it was justification for keeping Hudson alive awhile longer.

Laptop or not, he would eventually give up the codes, and when he did, he would get his reward, as promised.

Yi smiled at that thought and glanced again at his watch. Three minutes left.

Punta de las Sueños
Culiacán, Sinaloa, Mexico

BOLAN LOOKED AT the collection of dead bodies in the room, four in all, and the scattered bandages and first-aid patches on the three wounded marines.

"As you warned, my friend, they all went down hard." Martinez motioned toward the body of a dead female. "I feel bad that we had to kill her, but two of my marines hesitated and she shot them. As soldiers, as men, we stand ready to place our lives on the line. But a woman…" He shook his head.

"It doesn't sound like she gave you much choice," Bolan said. "What have you found out about her?"

"Her name was Kim Soo-Han. She is registered as being Chinese, with a Chinese passport, but upon closer inspection, I am certain that it will be shown to be a forgery, as will the passports of the others in her party."

"Where are they?" Bolan asked.

"They are gone. We are checking the airport now."

"She looks more Korean than Chinese," Grimaldi said.

"She had been seen in the company of an American named James Hudson," Martinez said. "He is among the registered guests for—" he paused to read from his pad "—the New International Independent Space Agency."

He flipped the pad closed. "Hudson is also among those listed as missing."

"Sounds like he was in on it," Grimaldi said.

"Who else is missing?" Bolan asked.

"In addition to the Chinese, two employees of the space agency company named Terrance Turner and Vassili Nabokovski. I have been told they are rocket scientists."

"That last name sounds Russian," Grimaldi said. "You sure he was with an American company?"

Martinez nodded. "That is the information I was given. The owner of the company was named Phillip McGreagor. His body was discovered in his suite, along with those of three men from one of the drug cartels. There are other cartel bodies on-site."

Bolan had heard of Phillip McGreagor, and pondered the situation. An American space-exploration company, two rocket scientists, one of whom was possibly Russian, and old Soviet-era missiles, all being sought by North Korea… Bolan didn't like the way this was shaping up.

He squatted to get a closer look at the dead woman.

Martinez's cell phone rang, and he stepped away to answer it.

Bolan lifted the woman's body slightly, noticing a black laptop underneath, her left hand still clutching it. He stood, looking around the room. The cabinet by the wall was standing open. Bolan saw that there was a room safe inside, the door of which was ajar.

"I'd like to get a look at that laptop," Bolan said to Grimaldi, taking out his sat phone. "Let's see if Hal can convince the State Department to work its magic and cut through some of the red tape."

He was about to call Brognola when Martinez said, *"Madre de Dios!"* As the sergeant pressed the phone to his ear, his mouth twisted into a frown. He ended the call and turned to Bolan.

"I have just been informed that a private jet left the airport two hours prior to your arrival. Its country of origin was Iran, and there was a group of Asians, a Russian and two Americans on board."

"What's their destination?" Bolan asked.

"It is listed as North Korea," Martinez said.

"Pyongyang?" Bolan asked.

Martinez shook his head. "No, Tang Hae Hong."

"Tang Hae Hong?" Grimaldi said. "Hey, isn't that the place where—"

"They launch their intercontinental ballistic missiles," Bolan said, finishing the sentence for him. He looked at Grimaldi. "Looks like we're going to North Korea."

Grimaldi raised both eyebrows. "Yeah, and we'd better hurry up. They've got a head start on us, and once they cross the international date line we'll be a whole day behind."

12

Osan Air Base
South Korea

Bolan shouldered his ditty bag as he and Grimaldi walked down the Jetway from the transport plane along with the group of arriving troops. They'd both used the seventeen-hour flight to get some much-needed sleep, but Bolan still felt restless. Their target's three-hour head start from Mexico had now stretched to a solid eight, and he had no doubt the Iranian ship with the missiles was probably close to, if not already in, North Korean territorial waters. He only hoped that Brognola had continued to use his influence and powers of persuasion on those in high places to grease the wheels here in Korea so they could hit the ground running. He decided to find out and reached for his sat phone.

Grimaldi slapped his shoulder and pointed to an Air Force Humvee heading across the tarmac. "I don't think you're going to have time to make that call, partner. Want to bet that's for us?"

Bolan held the phone down by his leg and watched as the Humvee swerved around the line of service person-

nel and screeched to a halt. An NCO who had been usher-
ing the soldiers and airmen off the plane barked an order
for the group to keep moving, did an about-face, came to
attention and whipped a salute. The door opened and a
fresh-faced second lieutenant jumped out and returned
the salute, still moving at a rapid walk.

"Which one of you is Cooper?" he asked.

"I am," Bolan said.

"I'm Lieutenant Beck." He extended his hand. "If you'll
step over to the vehicle, I'll take you to the briefing area."

Bolan slipped his phone into his pocket and walked toward the Humvee.

Grimaldi, following, said, "Hey, Lieu, that's not much
of a welcome to the Land of the Morning Calm."

The lieutenant's mouth twitched into a half grin. "It
might not be staying that way much longer. We're on alert."

Tang Hae Hong
North Korea

YI WATCHED AND listened as General Song described their
progress to their leader over the telephone. Song appeared
sober enough, but Yi could detect the vestiges of alcohol
seeping from his pores.

A wise general did not celebrate prematurely, he
thought. Song would do well to remember that lesson.

But soon it would not matter. With this magnificent success almost at hand, the completion of such an important
mission would certainly garner Yi a promotion. Soon he
would be Song's equal in rank. Then he would slowly expel
the drunken fool from any serious sphere of influence.

Yi turned to the large trucks that were pulling into place
on the concrete docks. The onboard cranes were already
hoisting the missiles out of the cargo hold to be transported
to the launch preparation site. He hoped the technology

they would provide, despite its antiquity, would be enough to bridge the final gap in his country's missile program. The two scientists would augment this function as well, now that they were guests of the Democratic People's Republic of Korea. But even with them, the NIISA computer plans for the long-range reentry system were imperative. He had to unscramble that final obstacle. Then Washington would soon be cowering under the threat of a nuclear launch that could reach not only their shores, but their precious White House, as well. It was the next step in the homeland becoming a new world superpower. Soon the Korean peninsula would no longer be divided, and the American imperialists would be driven from its shores.

Song finished his conversation and hung up. He strode over to Yi, his mouth working like a mouse nibbling on a kernel of rice.

"Why is it taking them so long to unload?" Song asked. "Our beloved leader has already made the announcement of an impending launch. I want the new missiles photographed."

"That was unwise," Yi said.

"What did you say?" Song said angrily.

"A wise man does not promise what he cannot deliver," Yi stated. "These missiles, this technology, must be examined and redesigned. You do not get a harvest of rice from a bag of seeds."

Song licked his lips. "Nonetheless, it is now time to bask in the glory of our coming greatness."

Yi nodded, saying nothing more. He had no time to deal with this simpleton.

"Our leader was very impressed with the extent of our success," Song said.

Our success? Yi resisted the urge to mention that it was his efforts, not Song's, that had assured the success of the mission.

"He wishes to view the fruits of our labors personally," Song said. "He will be on his way here shortly."

"What?"

Song looked as though it was he who was conversing with a simpleton. "I said that our leader is currently attending a commemorative event, and then he will be coming here."

Yi felt a shiver go up his spine. If the great one arrived, only to discover the reentry technology in an unreadable state, his anger would be immeasurable. Both Yi and Song would face firing squads.

Song smiled, his eyes turning into slits resembling those of a happy pig, unaware that he was marked for the slaughter. "He will be most impressed when he arrives."

Yi hadn't been expecting this so soon. He turned his head toward Song. "When is he due to arrive?"

"Tonight. He wishes not only to view our triumph firsthand, but also to lend his presence at the launching of the newest missile in defiance of the Americans." Song smiled again. "The preparations for the new missile launch have already begun."

Yi had no doubt that their leader, who had little patience and even less foresight, would fail to grasp that the real triumph here was the successful acquisition of the technology, which would eventually enable them to achieve their goals of interballistic accuracy upon reentry. But just as a spoiled, rich brat did not see the value in a bag of rice seeds, the temperamental man was used to immediate gratification. Yi recalled the execution of many members of the military high command who had dared give their leader an accurate assessment on the state of readiness of the missile systems.

"What time will he be here?" Yi asked.

Song shrugged. "As I said, he is at a commemorative event. Afterward, he will be under way."

That meant at least a few hours' respite. The image of their leader's frowning face again flashed through Yi's mind.

I must renew my efforts to break the American, he thought. I must decipher those encrypted files.

He took out his cell phone and punched in the number. The Dragon answered immediately.

"Have you taken them all to the appropriate location?" Yi asked.

"Not yet," the Dragon said. "I was awaiting your instructions."

"Do it. I will be along shortly."

He fingered the flash drive, as Hudson called it, in his pocket. The only task left to do now was the final, private interrogation of the hostages. Yi had lost all hope that Kim Soo-Han and the remaining Black Tigers had been successful in retrieving the laptop. Perhaps the two scientists could decipher the codes Hudson had placed on the flash drive. If not, Yi had to obtain that information from Hudson himself. Yi knew he would need one of his computer experts to assist. Lieutenant Ran would do nicely. Once the information was assessable, they could get rid of the American.

Everything—the ultimate success or failure of the mission, pleasing his leader, the promotion to general... Everything was now dependent on solving this one last problem.

Yi swallowed and looked at the grinning fool beside him.

If only he knew their lives were hanging in the balance...

Osan Air Base
South Korea

THE HUMVEE STOPPED in front of a building, and as they got out, Bolan glanced at a text he'd received from Brognola during the long flight: Laptop being examined. Belonged to James Hudson, NIISA security honcho. Also, Turner once worked for NASA. Classified government info may have been hacked. Will email you pics of each.

Grimaldi turned the phone so he could read it as well, after which he frowned and said, "This keeps getting better and better."

Bolan had surmised as much. But something else bothered him. If the North Koreans had already effected an escape from the resort in Mexico, and if they had the two rocket scientists as their prisoners, it made little sense to send a contingent back to the resort for a laptop.

Unless, he thought, there was some pretty significant information on it. Maybe they didn't have those top secret reentry plans after all. But then again, would they have departed without them?

Lieutenant Beck held the door and Bolan and Grimaldi entered the building. They were ushered down a hallway and into a room that had been darkened to accommodate the image on a large screen on the far wall.

It was obviously a satellite Skype hookup. The man on-screen sat up as they assembled in front of it.

Three men sat in chairs against the wall in the darkened room, off to the right.

"I'm Undersecretary William Howard," the oversize Skype image of a man said. "I assume you are both rested from your flight?"

Bolan felt little need for small talk. "Can you give us an update on the situation, sir?"

Howard blinked several times. He looked like a man who hadn't slept in days. "Well, first of all, the North Koreans have declared that us stopping and searching their cargo ship was an act of aggression. They're threatening to launch a missile in retaliation. We're got a naval destroyer in the area ready to shoot it down if it threatens the US."

"Have you got a fix on the Iranian ship and plane?" Bolan asked.

Howard's expression tightened and he nodded. "Both are in Tang Hae Hong, North Korea, at this time. We've been monitoring their activities via satellite. The ship's being unloaded as we speak."

"And the missiles were on board?" Bolan asked.

Howard nodded. "Yes, as we suspected. The plane, which has been identified as the same aircraft that left Culiacán Airport in Mexico, landed and was moved to a hangar."

"What's our plan?" Grimaldi asked. "After they stole those missiles from Panama, we're not going to let them get away with it, are we?"

"I'm afraid the situation is a bit more complex," Howard said. "At this point, I've been instructed to inform you that the missiles are no longer your concern."

"What?" Grimaldi exclaimed. "They get stopped in the Panama Canal with illegal cargo, ICBMs, no less, and then take them back by force, and we're going to twiddle our thumbs?"

"As I said," Howard continued, "the missiles are no longer your concern. Our main objective is to recover the hostages and any possible top secret technology that may have been compromised."

"Was there any indication of that on the laptop we recovered?" Bolan asked.

Howard compressed his lips, then nodded. "I'm afraid that a significant error was made in the sharing of sensitive information with the people at NIISA. One of the scientists, Dr. Turner, had worked in NASA for some time. He did have in his possession certain classified data, which he may have taken with him when he moved to NIISA. We're now concerned that some of these top secret files from NASA may have been inadvertently breached."

"You mean hacked?" Grimaldi asked. "What type of files?"

Howard paused, looked down and then took a deep breath. "Files related to reentry technology for long-range rockets."

"Or in the case of North Korea," Grimaldi said, "intercontinental ballistic missiles."

Howard said nothing.

"Marvelous." Grimaldi grunted. "You got any more good news?"

The undersecretary shook his head.

"Do you have any information regarding the hostages?" Bolan asked.

Howard nodded, looking as if he had a bad case of indigestion. "We've been monitoring things via satellite. The occupants of the plane, it appears, remained in the hangar for several hours. In the past twenty minutes, two vehicles pulled up to the entrance, and it looked as though three individuals were herded inside one of them, along with some apparent military personnel. We're tracking them now. We suspect they're heading for a remote battery encampment south of Tang Hae Hong and north of the DMZ."

"You have information as far as their identities?" Bolan asked.

"It's our conjecture, from what we've been able to piece together from the scene at the Mexican resort, that the three in custody are white males. Two Americans and one Russian national who was in the US on a work visa."

"Two rocket scientists and one slightly corrupt security consultant," Grimaldi said. "How soon can you get us a ride up to Tang Hae? And what kind of backup are we getting?"

Howard started to speak, but was interrupted as one of the men sitting off to the side stood and said, "That's my department, son."

As the figure stepped out of the shadows, he was partially illuminated by the glow from the screen. Bolan saw he was a rugged-looking guy in his fifties with iron-gray hair clipped very short and a lieutenant colonel's black oak-leaf insignia on his uniform. The dark stitching above his pocket identified him as Johnson, US Army. A green beret was folded and tucked under his belt, and his patches and combat-infantry badge told Bolan all that he needed to know. He extended his hand. "Glad to meet you, Colonel."

The colonel shook Bolan's hand and then Grimaldi's. Turning, Johnson motioned for the other seated men to come forward. One guy was an American who looked to be in his midthirties. His uniform bore the same Special Forces insignias and beret as Johnson's, except that his rank was an E-7.

"This is Sergeant Wilson," the colonel said. "His squad will be assisting you. As observers."

"Observers?" Grimaldi repeated with a grin.

Wilson winked as he shook hands with Bolan and Grimaldi.

An Asian of about the same age stood next to Wilson, but his uniform had no insignias, name or rank. He stepped forward, offering his hand.

"I am Mr. Park," he said. "With what you Americans call the Korean CIA. I will be accompanying you on the trip to the North, as well."

Bolan nodded as he sized up the new guys. They both looked combat hardened and formidable. "I take it this won't be the first such trip for either of you?" he asked.

"It will almost be like going home again," Park said. "My grandfather was born in Pyongyang."

"How rough is it usually?" Grimaldi asked.

"Making the trip there is easy. Getting back alive is the tricky part."

Military bunker
South of Tang Hae Hong, North Korea

JAMES HUDSON LAY on the concrete floor in the dark, windowless room, alone and unable to feel his arms or hands. He was unsure how much time had passed. The ropes binding him had cut off most, if not all, of his circulation. His face and body felt sore from the beating administered back at the airport in Mexico after they'd discovered the files were encrypted. He'd held out as long as he could, hoping that Soo-Han would somehow intercede and save him. But he quickly realized that wasn't going to happen when he kept catching glimpses of her sitting impassively and watching as the Dragon delivered blow after calculated blow. They were designed to create pain—sharp, twisting pain—but allow him to remain conscious. The guy was a monster. Finally, at the urging of both Turner and Nabokovski, who probably were worried they'd be next, he'd broken, spilling the beans about the passwords on the laptop.

"I couldn't recall them if my life depended on it," he'd said.

Yi had grabbed a handful of Hudson's hair and twisted his head up and around so their eyes met.

"Your life does depend on it," the colonel said.

He'd sent Soo-Han back to the resort to get the laptop, and she hadn't returned. They'd taken off without her, which most likely meant that she was either in police custody or dead. Maybe the Mexican cops had found out, or maybe more of the cartel goons had grabbed her. Hudson didn't want to think about that. He still had vestiges of feeling for her, even though she'd proved less than loyal to him.

More time passed, and Hudson heard what he thought sounded like a helicopter. The sound grew closer and then ceased.

Had someone landed a craft here? And what did that mean for him?

He got his answer a few minutes later when the door on the far wall opened and three men stepped inside. They closed the door and switched on the light. When his eyes adjusted to the brightness, Hudson recognized two of them immediately: Yi and the Dragon. The third man was clad in a military uniform and wore glasses. His face was slender and waspish looking, and he held a laptop.

"Jimmy," Yi said with derision, "I hope you are well rested."

Hudson saw the Dragon's face break into a smile as he stared down at him.

"This is Lieutenant Ran," Yi said, pointing to the man with the glasses. The colonel held up the flash drive. "He is here to assist you in the retrieval of the files."

Ran's expression was all business.

"Untie me," Hudson managed to say. "Please. I can't help you like this."

The three Koreans stood silent for a few seconds, and then Yi motioned to the Dragon. He moved forward and lifted Hudson to his feet, as easily as if he were picking up a sack of potatoes.

Hudson's mind raced on how he might be able to delay things, forestall the inevitable that he knew was coming.

Demilitarized Zone
The 38th Parallel

THE FOUR MEN crouched in the darkness of the dense undergrowth, approximately one hundred yards from the long cyclone fence that marked the southern border of the DMZ.

"This is strictly a black ops operation," Wilson said, his face now painted black with green stripes. He had shed his standard military uniform for the same black BDUs that Bolan, Grimaldi and Park were wearing. "I've got my men standing by in support positions, but officially we're not here." A glimpse of white teeth flashed under his bushy mustache.

"My men, as well," Park said, tapping his earpiece receptor. "We are all ghosts now."

"Yeah? How are we going to get across the DMZ?" Grimaldi asked. "It's some of the most heavily mined real estate in the world, isn't it?"

"You are right," Park said. "We won't go across. We'll go under."

"For several generations now," Wilson said, "the North Koreans have been building tunnels underneath the DMZ in anticipation of an invasion of the South. We've been discovering and monitoring them, and eventually placing obstacles inside, like booby-traps, or blowing them up. But a few we've left intact so we can pay some visits of our own occasionally."

"This one is mostly okay," Park said. "We have blocked the exit with many kilos of rock and dirt, but we have our own tunnel next to it, so we can still use it."

"They're breaking through now," Wilson said. "Once we gain access we'll have a quick trek under the Zee, and then about ten klicks to get to this bunker where our intel believes they've got the hostages stashed."

Bolan nodded. "Ten klicks is a long haul."

Wilson grinned again. "Park's operatives have already procured a couple of vehicles for that purpose. One military, one civilian. There's a road we can take. The only trouble is, there's very little traffic along the highways up there. Hardly anyone has a vehicle, much less money for gas."

"Great, so we'll be sitting ducks," Grimaldi said.

"Well," Wilson replied, "I never said it was going to be a cakewalk."

"Meanwhile," Park said, pulling a burlap sack and a roll of duct tape out of his ditty bag, "we must tape these over the ejection ports of our weapons."

"Why?" Grimaldi asked.

"It's SOP for operations in the DMZ," Wilson said. "The North Koreans do the same thing. No one can leave any traceable shell casings."

Park reached for Grimaldi's MP-5. "I have a smaller bag for your pistol."

Bolan unslung his weapon and took one of the bags. It was porous enough to allow the expended gas to dissipate, but sturdy enough to catch any expelled rounds.

"Doesn't this increase the chance the weapon will jam?" Bolan asked.

Park nodded. "Sorry 'bout that, but we must leave nothing behind. Not even one shell casing."

Bolan nodded and handed Park the weapon. The Executioner was already reprioritizing the mission mentally. Although Wilson hadn't said so, he was certain some Special Forces snipers would set up to provide up-to-date intel.

Park's head jerked as he obviously received a transmission on his radio. He muttered a response and turned to Bolan.

"It is time," he said.

Military bunker
South of Tang Hae Hong, North Korea

YI WATCHED AS the Dragon bent Hudson's left hand back and then grabbed his smallest finger. The man groaned in pain as the Dragon glanced at Yi, who nodded.

With a deft movement, the Dragon bent the finger all the way back, causing the American to cry out.

The colonel nodded again, and the Dragon let the American fall to his knees. The two scientists, sitting on a cot, looked away.

Breaking a man was done in stages. Yi knew that from many years of practice. A prisoner needed to be given an interim between inflicted injuries to reflect on what was yet to come.

Yi was impressed by Hudson's resistance. Despite several attempts in which he feigned cooperation, only to turn away after a plethora of failed efforts to open the files, they were no closer now than when they had begun several hours prior.

Even Ran's continued efforts to unlock the mystery had garnered them nothing. He sat in front of the laptop in frustration.

And now Hudson was once again professing ignorance as to the passwords needed to decode the computer files. Even after escalating sessions of physical persuasion, the American's story had not altered; he needed the laptop. Yi began to worry as he glanced at his watch. Four hours had passed since he'd transported the guests of his nation to this bunker, hoping to retrieve the files so that they could be presented to his leader upon his arrival. Yi wondered when that would be. He debated calling Song and informing him of the situation, telling him that he needed a bit more time to set everything up… But the drunken fool, Yi knew, would only place all the blame on him, taking none of the responsibility himself.

No, the only course now was to extract the information. They had to break the American.

Yi's cell phone rang and he answered it.

"This is General Song," the voice said. "Where are you, and where are the Americans?"

"I am conducting my final interrogation," Yi said.

"Well, hurry up." Song's voice was ripe with anger, impatience. "Our great leader is about to arrive."

Yi muttered a reply and terminated the call. As he put his cell phone back in its holder, he stared down at Hudson, who was cowering on the floor.

"It seems as though time has run out for both of us," Yi said, removing his pistol from its holster. "You will tell us how to open the files now or you will die."

WILSON HANDED BOLAN the night-vision binoculars. The Executioner adjusted the zoom button and scanned the front of the bunker, which was little more than forty yards away. It was a long rectangular brick building with thin slits for windows. Each one was blacked out, showing no trace of illumination from inside. The door looked to be solid steel, which made the possibility of a physical breach a bit of a challenge. Bolan swept the area. The green image showed three soldiers wearing the same dark BDUs as the ones they'd tangled with in Cuba. They were lounging at their posts, looking as if they had dropped their guard since arriving back in their own country.

"Looks like the same outfit," he said.

"North Korean special forces," Wilson said. "They call them the Black Tigers. Pretty rough sons of bitches."

"They look relaxed." Bolan handed the binoculars to Grimaldi.

"Hell, they're probably as exhausted from all this as we are," the Stony Man pilot said.

"Looks like two sentries guarding the building, and one on the chopper," Wilson whispered.

"Yeah," Grimaldi said. "And that helicopter looks like an Mi-24 Hind. Plenty of room. If it's got enough fuel, I can fly us all out of here in style."

"We've got our exit plan in place," Wilson stated. "I'd suggest we don't deviate from it."

"Let's keep an open mind," Bolan said. "Our next objective is taking out the sentries in a timely fashion."

Wilson keyed his mic and said, "Whenever you're ready."

Bolan nodded and Wilson whispered, "It's a go."

The Executioner watched as two of Park's men, about twenty-five yards away, rose and fired their sound-suppressed MP-5s. As if on cue, all three sentries collapsed. But Bolan was already moving. Surprise was their greatest ally in an attack, and he had no doubt that the interior would hold more obstacles.

Knowing that Grimaldi, Wilson and Park were right behind him, Bolan covered the distance to the bunker just as two of Park's men set off an explosive charge that blew the solid steel door inward. The interior was well lit, and Bolan could see hurried movement inside the first room. He pulled the pin from the stun grenade he'd been gripping, and tossed it through the opening. Flattening himself against the wall, he waited the intervening few seconds for the blast. The concussive wave blew debris out the doorway, and Bolan wheeled inside, his MP-5 ready.

Two more Black Tigers stumbled toward him, trying to bring up their AK-47s. The Executioner zipped a three-round burst into each man's chest, and they tumbled forward as the burlap bag taped to his weapon puffed up like a balloon, then slowly started to deflate.

The room narrowed to a hallway, which Bolan knew could quickly become a kill zone. There were four doors on each side. Another Black Tiger appeared from a room at the end of the corridor. Before the man could fire his raised weapon, Bolan shot him. Then he pulled another stun grenade from his pants pocket, snagged the pin and yanked it free. Releasing the flange, Bolan silently counted off three seconds, then tossed the device underhanded down the hallway.

It exploded seconds later as he made it to the closest door. Bolan took a look inside, while Grimaldi, Wilson and Park raced past him on their way to clear the other rooms. Through the haze of swirling dust, Bolan saw that the space contained five men in various positions. One in civilian clothes lay on the floor. A uniformed soldier holding a pistol stood over him. Another uniformed soldier was trying to stand, black-framed glasses askew on his face. He held a laptop against his body with his left hand, a pistol in his right. Bolan shot him, and he twisted and fell. Two more men, who looked to be Turner and Nabokovski, sat on a cot, their legs shackled.

The surviving soldier, an officer by the look of him, turned and pointed his gun at the Executioner. A three-round burst from Bolan's MP-5 dropped him. The Executioner moved forward, sweeping the area as he went, but the inflated burlap bag impeded his view. Abruptly, he felt a powerful kick knock him back against the wall. He tried to bring the MP-5 around to fire at his assailant, a solidly built Korean, but the bag had become snarled in the weapon's slide, causing a jam.

Bolan grabbed the cocking lever to clear the machine gun, but the Korean was too quick. He grabbed the barrel and the stock and tried to twist the weapon out of Bolan's hands. The Executioner responded with a knee to the other man's groin, but his aim was slightly off. When he kneed his attacker's abdomen, it felt like a tree trunk. He felt his back strike the wall again as his opponent surged forward, then kicked him in the stomach and rolled backward, executing a judo throw. Bolan sailed through the air and then landed hard on the floor.

He felt the jammed weapon being ripped from his grasp. The Korean tore at the bag, attempting to clear the blockage, but Bolan lashed out with his right foot and kicked the MP-5 from his adversary's hands. He rolled to his feet and felt a sharp pain in his left knee as the Korean's instep slammed into it. Bolan's leg gave out, sending him to the floor.

The other man leaped forward, sending a stomping blow toward Bolan's head. The Executioner managed to dodge it, his ear only inches from the hard slap of the other man's boot on the concrete.

Bolan used his momentum to roll left. He was on all fours, about to regain his footing, when he felt the sharp pain of a front kick in his rib cage. Staggering backward, he raised his arms just in time to block a vicious round-house kick aimed at his head. He brought his elbow down on the Korean's thigh, causing him to recoil, but if he'd felt the blow, his face did not show it.

The Korean assumed a classic fighting stance, and Bolan did the same. The other man's left foot whipped forward in a front kick, and when Bolan lowered his arm to block it, the Korean pivoted and transformed the kick into another roundhouse, smacking into Bolan's face. The Executioner staggered back a step, his opponent pressing forward. In a split second, Bolan saw an opening and sent a quick, hard jab into the Korean's face. His head snapped back, minimizing the blow, but Bolan stepped forward and delivered a straight right that knocked the man backward.

The Korean recovered quickly, and his gaze shifted to the MP-5, which lay a few feet away.

In a split second both men rushed for it, grabbing the weapon and struggling for a dominant grip. Their bodies crashed together and they fell in a heap, with the Korean twisting so that he landed on top. Bolan jerked the weapon free as his adversary struggled to regain his grasp, and tore the burlap bag away from the ejection port, the remnants of the tape sagging downward.

He rolled away from the Korean, brought the barrel around and pulled the trigger, firing a three-round burst into the man's chest. He collapsed to the floor, dead.

"The rest of the building is clear," Wilson said as Bolan got to his feet.

"Looks like we have to police some brass," Park said, bending to pick up the expended shell casings from the MP-5.

"Be my guest," Bolan said.

Park immediately began to check the bodies, kicking away any weapons he found. He turned over the corpse of Bolan's hand-to-hand opponent and stepped back in surprise.

"This is Gumon Yoong," Park said. "He is called the Black Dragon."

"He's the Dead Dragon now," Grimaldi said.

The pilot went to the two men shackled to the cot. He knelt and examined them. "You guys all right?"

"You're an American?" one asked.

Grimaldi nodded.

"Thank God," the man said.

"This is Colonel Yi Sun-Shin," Park said, examining the uniformed officer Bolan had shot.

"This one's still alive," Wilson said, helping the man on the floor to sit up.

Bolan recognized him as James Hudson.

Hudson managed to raise what appeared to be a shattered hand. "Get that flash drive." He pointed to the piece of red plastic extending from the laptop in the grasp of the third dead North Korean soldier.

Grimaldi scooted across the floor and snatched it, then took the laptop, as well.

"We must recover all the brass and remove the bodies," Park said, patting the burlap sack taped to his weapon. "Bury them. Your grenade fragments, as well. As I said, no one must know we were here."

"Hell," Grimaldi said. "Why not just load 'em in the helicopter and drop them somewhere discreet?"

Park glanced at Wilson, who in turn looked at Bolan. "Well, we had another exit planned, but…"

"Why crawl when you can fly?" Grimaldi asked.

Bolan glanced at his watch. "May I suggest we seriously consider that suggestion before any more Black Tigers happen our way?"

"That sounds like a good plan," Park said with a grin. "If they see it's one of theirs, they probably won't fire on us. And we don't have to go through that damn tunnel again."

Epilogue

Stony Man Farm
Virginia

The image on the big screen in Brognola's office showed a fiery explosion as a missile lifted off the launch pad, hesitated and fell downward, causing an even greater blast.

"So much for the glorious leader's latest missile threat," Brognola said with a grin.

He poured two cups of coffee, walked over and set them in front of Bolan and Grimaldi. "Mr. Hudson's in custody and being charged with numerous crimes and misdemeanors, and both of the rocket scientists are recovering nicely. You guys did a hell of job."

"We didn't recover the missiles the Black Tigers stole from Panama," Bolan said. He hated leaving any part of a job undone.

"Actually," Brognola said, leaning forward, "this was one time we really did cover all the bases. Unbeknownst to almost everyone, the Agency sent a team down to Panama shortly after the missiles were originally seized." He paused to pick up his own mug and took a sip. "As you know, fifty-plus years ago the Soviets took all the nuclear triggers out of them, and I was recently informed our guys removed all the guidance systems from the old missiles. The ones the North Koreans and the Iranians got were just old hollow shells."

"So that's why our undersecretary of defense was so adamant about not worrying about the missiles?" Bolan asked.

Brognola nodded.

"It would have been nice of them to tell us beforehand," Grimaldi said.

"Well, you know I always say that the left hand doesn't know what the right hand's doing," Brognola mused. "This was just another example of it."

The Executioner remained silent, thinking about the challenges of his never-ending war. This time things had worked out for the good guys. What would tomorrow bring? He had no idea, but he would be ready to face it head-on—as always.

* * * * *

UPCOMING TITLES FROM

THE Executioner _DON PENDLETON'S_

TERRORIST DISPATCH – _Don Pendleton_
Available September 2016

Atrocities continue in the Ukraine and the
adjoining Crimean Peninsula, annexed by
Russia in March 2014. With no end in sight,
a plan is hatched to force American
involvement by sending Ukrainian militants
to strike Washington, DC, killing civilians
and seizing the Lincoln Memorial as protest
against their homeland's threat from Russia.
Can Bolan bring the war home to the plotters'
doorstep?

COMBAT MACHINES – _Don Pendleton_
Available December 2016

What began in a Romanian orphanage twenty
years earlier, when a man walked away with ten
children and disappeared, leads Mack Bolan
and a team of Interpol agents to fend off a
group of "invisible" assassins carving their way
across Europe...toward the USA.

REQUEST YOUR FREE BOOKS!
2 FREE NOVELS PLUS 2 FREE GIFTS!

ℍ HARLEQUIN®

INTRIGUE

BREATHTAKING ROMANTIC SUSPENSE

YES! Please send me 2 FREE Harlequin® Intrigue novels and my 2 FREE gifts (gifts are worth about $10). After receiving them, if I don't wish to receive any more books, I can return the shipping statement marked "cancel." If I don't cancel, I will receive 6 brand-new novels every month and be billed just $4.74 per book in the U.S. or $5.49 per book in Canada. That's a savings of at least 12% off the cover price! It's quite a bargain! Shipping and handling is just 50¢ per book in the U.S. and 75¢ per book in Canada.* I understand that accepting the 2 free books and gifts places me under no obligation to buy anything. I can always return a shipment and cancel at any time. Even if I never buy another book, the two free books and gifts are mine to keep forever.

182/382 HDN GH3D

Name	(PLEASE PRINT)

Address	Apt. #

City	State/Prov.	Zip/Postal Code

Signature (if under 18, a parent or guardian must sign)

Mail to the **Reader Service:**
IN U.S.A.: P.O. Box 1867, Buffalo, NY 14240-1867
IN CANADA: P.O. Box 609, Fort Erie, Ontario L2A 5X3
**Are you a subscriber to Harlequin® Intrigue books
and want to receive the larger-print edition?
Call 1-800-873-8635 or visit www.ReaderService.com.**

* Terms and prices subject to change without notice. Prices do not include applicable taxes. Sales tax applicable in N.Y. Canadian residents will be charged applicable taxes. Offer not valid in Quebec. This offer is limited to one order per household. Not valid for current subscribers to Harlequin Intrigue books. All orders subject to credit approval. Credit or debit balances in a customer's account(s) may be offset by any other outstanding balance owed by or to the customer. Please allow 4 to 6 weeks for delivery. Offer available while quantities last.

Your Privacy—The Reader Service is committed to protecting your privacy. Our Privacy Policy is available online at www.ReaderService.com or upon request from the Reader Service.

We make a portion of our mailing list available to reputable third parties that offer products we believe may interest you. If you prefer that we not exchange your name with third parties, or if you wish to clarify or modify your communication preferences, please visit us at www.ReaderService.com/consumerschoice or write to us at Reader Service Preference Service, P.O. Box 9062, Buffalo, NY 14240-9062. Include your complete name and address.

HII5

Bolan perched atop a seven-story office building opposite
The Hungry Wolf, with a clear view inside the restaurant
through two large plate-glass windows. Peering through
the Leupold sight mounted on his Remington bolt-action
rifle, he felt almost like a guest invited to the party,
moving in among the four- and six-man tables, touching-
close but unseen by the men whose night he meant to
spoil.

For some, it would be their last night on Earth.

The Model 700 was not designed with war in mind,
though it held four .300 Winchester Magnum rounds, one
in the chamber and three in a round-hinged floorplate
magazine. Its barrel measured twenty-four inches and
could send a 220-grain bullet downrange at a velocity of
2,850 feet per second, striking with 3,908 foot-pounds of
cataclysmic energy.

All good news for a sniper on the go.

Bolan had been in place awhile, spotting the restaurant's
arrivals as they entered, scanning faces already seated
at tables when he took his post. Stepan Melnyk was
nowhere to be seen, but Dmytro Levytsky was making
the rounds, slapping shoulders and laughing at jokes
from his soldiers, here and there bending to whisper in

ears. A maître d' in a tuxedo loitered on the sidelines, muttering to waiters as they passed, dispersing drinks and appetizers. No one on the staff looked happy to be there, but they were working quietly, efficiently, focused entirely on the task at hand, avoiding eye contact with any of their customers.

Bolan did not plan a sustained attack his first time out, but he had four spare cartridges lined up beside him on the rooftop, or a quick reload if time allowed. The shooting would be loud, and there'd be no mistaking it for anything mundane, such as a vehicle's backfire in the street. Once he began, there'd be no stopping until Bolan disengaged and fled the scene, hopefully well ahead of any armed pursuit.

He scoped the two hardmen on the entrance first, decided not to kill them yet and let the Leupold scope take him inside The Hungry Wolf. He felt that way himself when it was time to thin the herd of savages who preyed on so-called civilized society. He wasn't bloodthirsty and hadn't killed out of anger since the first strike that avenged his family, many years ago, but there was no denying that eliminating vicious predators lifted a weight from Bolan's soul, if only temporarily.

So many goons, so little time.

He chose a laughing face at random, framed it with the Leupold's reticle, inhaled and let half of the breath escape as he squeezed the trigger.

Don't miss
TERRORIST DISPATCH by Don Pendleton,
available September 2016 wherever
Gold Eagle® books and ebooks are sold.

REQUEST YOUR FREE BOOKS!
2 FREE NOVELS PLUS 2 FREE GIFTS!

H HARLEQUIN®

ROMANTIC suspense

Sparked by danger, fueled by passion